Florida

Journeys

Florida

Journeys

by
Daniel Hance Page

SEAWORTHY PUBLICATIONS, INC. • MELBOURNE, FLORIDA

Florida Journeys
Copyright ©2021 by Daniel Hance Page

Published in the USA and distributed worldwide by:
Seaworthy Publications, Inc.
6300 N. Wickham Rd
Unit 130-416
Melbourne, FL 32940
Phone 310-610-3634
Email orders@seaworthy.com
www.seaworthy.com

The cover painting of a tranquil Florida beach scene that adorns this book was painted by Tommaso Di Raimondo, an Italian painter currently living in Germany where he has his own fine art atelier and works in oils, watercolors, and tempera. His web site is: www.TommasoDiRaimondo.com

Library of Congress Cataloging-in-Publication Data

Names: Page, Daniel H., 1943- author.
Title: Florida journeys / by Daniel Hance Page.
Description: Melbourne, Florida : Seaworthy Publications, 2021. | Summary:
  "Daniel Hance Page enjoys telling stories with a message to be
  considered. Florida Journeys is a two-part book that talks about how
  people's lives are interwoven in the backdrop of the warm Florida
  climate. In Part I of this two-part book, "Gone Fishing, A Journey of No
  Return," Rintin Fox is about to take a journey that will forever change
  his life. He is living a typical 9 to 5 existence and feels like
  something is missing. He gets no pleasure from anything and when his
  outdoors-loving girlfriend finally dumps him, he decides to go to
  Florida and learn to fish. It becomes a journey of introspection from
  which there truly is no return. In Part II - "Lost No Longer," we have a
  different kind of journey into self-preservation and survival. Benteen
  (Ben) Sands thinks he is going on a Florida holiday. But due to a
  robbery and fearing for his life, he runs far into the Florida outback
  where he becomes hopelessly lost and must find his way back to
  civilization. He first finds ways to survive, then eventually finds his
  way back. Returning to civilization, he becomes a sort of
  quasi-celebrity known as The Wild Man or The Man with the Spear." But
  even though he returns to civilization, the wild is now a part of him.
  Eventually, he is drawn back to the home he built in the wild where he
  finds his destiny"-- Provided by publisher.
Identifiers: LCCN 2021005056 (print) | LCCN 2021005057 (ebook) | ISBN
  9781948494519 (paperback) | ISBN 9781948494526 (ebook)
Subjects: LCSH: Self-realization--Fiction. | Florida--Fiction.
Classification: LCC PS3616.A3374 F57 2021 (print) | LCC PS3616.A3374
  (ebook) | DDC 813/.6--dc23
LC record available at https://lccn.loc.gov/2021005056
LC ebook record available at https://lccn.loc.gov/2021005057

Dedication

Marg, Hank, Jim, Ivadelle, Sheldon, Colleen, Shane and Shannon Page, John, Dan and the Robinson family, Lester and Rose Anderson, Doug, Don, Bob Sephton and families, Garry and the Pratt family, the Massey family, Murray, Sue and the Shearer family, Joe and Linda Hill, Macari Bishara, Joan LeBoeuf, Kevin, Alison and Michaela Griffin, Jerry and Gaye McFarland, Dr. David and June Chambers, "Mac" McCormick, Grant Saunders, Frank Lewis and other friends with whom we have enjoyed the wilderness.

"For there is another kingdom
beneath the water deep and blue,
where the treasures of the sea
are only discovered by a certain few."
Moonstar

"Gather memories to last forever-
that you may revisit often when you dream."
Moonstar

"Rise free from care before the dawn, and seek adventures.
Let the moon find thee by other lakes, and the night overtake thee
everywhere at home."
Henry David Thoreau

PART ONE

GONE FISHING,
A JOURNEY OF NO RETURN

Chapter One
Setting Out

Rinton Fox, known mainly as Rin, sat back in a comfortable chair next to a tall, snapping, and fragrant fire to watch people at the party. Then suddenly he realized he wasn't just watching others because he realized he was in fact observing his own life. Looking back, one struggle had led to another bringing him to this night. For a moment, at least, he declared, I would like to stop the struggle and try to see a purpose. Rather than just enduring events, as in the past, I would like to try to enjoy them and see life, no longer as an endurance contest but as an opportunity. This party might be my chance to change. I would also like to stop being just a watcher of life or a struggling survivor and become a person on a quest—a searcher. So far I have accomplished little, although I have friends at this party as well as my girlfriend, Amber Carlson.

As Rin's thoughts settled on Amber, she stepped into the light from the fire and started talking to another woman. Amber had short, black hair. Her eyes were also black and showed a depth of character along with fire. She was slim and tall. Her fine facial features had clear, direct beauty, seeming to reflect the surroundings where she lived, for mainly she likes fishing and is a guide.

We actually have little in common, thought Rin in a flash of hard honesty. She seeks a life of fishing. This quest takes her to beautiful places with rivers and lakes. I'm a city guy and work in an office. I'm a business manager and like to live in a controlled environment—not dependent on constantly changing weather.

Amber stepped toward Rin, noting as she saw him that his appearance was more rugged than his lifestyle. All the features of his face were strong, centering on his eyes that were brown. Noting his gray hair, she thought he'd better do something with his life before it's over. "Why don't you get up and do something?" she asked, not intending to sound so critical.

"Possibly," he countered, "I've done more, or accomplished more, sitting here than I have through much of my actions in the past."

"I just noticed your gray hair," again not intending to be so direct. "About time you accomplished something."

"I think I've just decided to change course," he explained. "Instead of just watching or enduring life, I'm going to try to enjoy it and see it as an opportunity. Next, though I need a purpose—or a quest."

"Go fishing," she declared. "I've been telling you that since we first met. Over and over again I've tried to get you out of your office— your indoor life—and see some of the beauty in the world that I see particularly when I'm fishing. Fishing is a way of life—if you could only see it. Maybe I've just had too much wine. But it hasn't changed me—only released me from my restrictions and left me honest. I've tried to change you and you won't change. As usual, I'm going to be the one to actually do something. I'm going to leave you until you discover who you are. I think I know but only you can decide. My advice to you now is the same as it's always been and that's go fishing. You might learn something. At least you will see what I've been trying to get you to understand since I met you. I'm going to leave you until you find out who you are. When you make this discovery, and you still want to look me up, I'd like to meet you."

Finishing these declarations, Amber walked out of the firelight and strode directly to her car. She drove out the driveway and her vehicle gradually became concealed by shadows.

Shocked, Rin watched the area where Amber had vanished. Continuing to focus on the place where he had lost so much, he thought the one accomplishment I had made in my life has just left—and I have no ride home.

He finished the beer he had been drinking then walked to the cooler and removed two more bottles. Slipping one into his pocket, he twisted the cap off the other, took a long drink then started walking. I could get a ride, he told himself, but I'd have to explain my situation and I don't understand it. When I was reflecting upon my life in a moment of clarity, I suddenly got thrust into a situation where I have nothing left but some advice—go fishing. I might learn something. All the time I've known Amber I've heard that advice. Since it's now all I have left I'll take it. I'll go fishing.

Walking along the side of the road in the darkness of night lit only by a shadowy moon and occasional lights from passing vehicles, Rin thought, my surroundings are much like the present condition of my life—darkness lit by very few bright spots. I've struggled—endured—and gained almost nothing. I won't cry about what I don't have. I'll work with what I continue to possess such as health and maybe other things. Amber gave me some advice and I think I'll follow it—and go fishing. I'll plan for a trip of indefinite length. Arrangements will have to be made about my apartment, work, and finances.

CHAPTER TWO
JOURNEY SOUTH

"The last thing my girlfriend said to me was, 'Go fishing. You might learn something,'" Rin said to the woman sitting next to him on the plane while they both sipped beer. She had brown hair with blonde streaks, bluish-gray eyes, a delicate nose, and lips—all conveying beauty at first although underlying roughness gradually tarnished the first impression. She also seemed friendly and talkative.

"I've heard of people being told to go and do a lot of things," she replied, "but this is the first time I've heard of someone being told to go fishing."

"Wasn't unusual for her," he countered, "because she likes to fish as often as possible. She is a guide herself and also books trips as a client with other guides. She has always been annoyed by my lack of interest in something she loves."

"I haven't often heard of women being fishing guides," she noted.

"Many get hooked more deeply than men," he affirmed.

"What interests you?" she asked.

"I'm a painter and photographer," he answered. "Most of my career has been centered on office work. And your interests?"

"Physiotherapist," she said.

"What's your name?" he asked.

"Flora—actually Florida," she answered. "This name was first given by the Spanish to the region as La Florida, the Land of Flowers. My favorite flower is oleander. I often wear one in my hair. I'm Flora Chase."

"I'm Rin," he said. "Rinton Fox."

"I've always liked foxes," she replied, smiling.

"Well thanks," he exclaimed. "I've always liked you too ever since I first met you."

"For about a whole hour actually," she stated.

"Yeah," he replied. "And they all said we wouldn't last."

"We've proven them wrong," she said, clinking her beer against his raised can.

"I knew we'd last," he boasted.

"I wish you a good fishing trip," she added.

"Fishing on the plane has been great," he said.

"And what have you caught?" she asked.

"The best catch I've had since the previous one got away," he answered.

"First I'm called a flower and now a fish," she said.

"Both are intended as compliments," he added.

"Good," she exclaimed. "Where are you going in Florida?"

"I was told to go fishing so I've booked a room on a beach resort and plan to try fishing with a charter boat. If you would like to come, I will enjoy your company until you decide to unhook yourself."

"I'll let you know when I'm unhooked," she said before a flight attendant brought them more drinks.

"Enjoying your flight?" asked the attendant who was neatly dressed with her blondish hair combed back from a finely featured face where pale blue eyes seemed to look at life with a gaze that portrayed years of experience.

"Life is better in the air than on the land," answered Rin. "On land, no one brings me drinks."

"That's your standard for a good life?" asked the attendant.

"It's a good start," he said. "And maybe that's what is happening now—for all of us."

"Thanks for the good news," she added before moving to the next passengers.

"If you're starting a good life," said Flora, "maybe I'll take you to the dog races and I'll share your winnings."

"You've got to have faith," stated Rin. "You go to the races?"

"Whenever possible," she noted after sipping more of the cold drink.

"Maybe this is all part of a good fishing trip," observed Rin.

"When making bets," explained Flora, "I don't rely on statistics. I work more on mood, hunches, and inspiration—and I win more than lose. The only bets I make are for the trifecta whereby you pick the first three finishers listed in the correct order of first, second, and third. Depending on the odds, a two-dollar bet can win hundreds or even beyond a thousand dollars." After removing pieces of paper and pens from her carry-on bag then giving one of each to Rin, she continued, "I'm going to pick my trifecta numbers for each race now and maybe you would like to do the same."

"You have got to have faith," replied Rin, accepting the paper and pen then starting to select numbers.

"Keep thinking about your choices until you feel they are right," she added.

They worked in silence while outside their window the setting sun painted clouds with golden tints. Colors darkened as night approached. Murkiness was dispelled when the cloud-strewn sky received shades of silver from a rising moon.

"You have your numbers?" she asked.

"Yes," he noted.

"All you have to do now is plan how you will spend your winnings," she explained, smiling.

"I've already spent them," he acknowledged.

"You've rented a car?" she asked.

"One is reserved," he said.

"You've booked a room?" she checked again.

"Yes," he replied. "I've also booked a trip with a charter fishing boat. The captain is Len Jackson."

"Have you met him?" she enquired again.

"No," he replied. "I found him online and booked a trip."

"First—the dog races?" she asked.

"Okay," he confirmed.

With a plan made, they rested quietly and were jolted back to a schedule when lights appeared outside the window. An attendant said to fasten seat belts to prepare for arrival in Florida.

The plane bumped the runway slightly while rejoining the ground. The craft stopped then action commenced as passengers prepared for disembarking. In the terminal, Flora and Rin collected their checked bags before walking to the car-rental booth.

In a short time lights from the airport were left behind as Rin drove toward the racetrack while Flora outlined the route. At the track, they made sure the car was locked then walked to the building.

Having made bets for each race, Rin and Flora purchased hot dogs and beer before selecting seats.

"Hot dogs are as delicious as they are unhealthy," observed Rin after the snacks had been enjoyed.

"We don't have time to get a healthy meal," explained Flora. "Beer is healthy except for the alcohol."

"We could keep the plastic cups for souvenirs," suggested Rin.

"At the end of the night we'll have lots of souvenirs—and extra cash," offered Flora.

"You have to have faith," added Rin.

They sipped beer contentedly while waiting and enjoying the night. The track was well lit. Leaves of palms rattled in a slight breeze. Snowy egrets stalked grass at the center of the field.

Rin was almost asleep, or at least completely rested, when he was jolted back to the race by a tumult of dogs as they bolted into a wild scramble with every muscle working at full capacity in a cloud of heads, bodies, and legs. Gradually the cloud lengthened into a thinning line of running forms. The race was fascinating although ultimately disappointing when the numbers of the first three dogs across the finish line did not match the bets. Caught by the moment, Rin walked downstairs, made additional bets then returned carrying two more cups of beer.

"Thank you," she exclaimed, receiving one of the cold, plastic cups. "I knew I was right to bring you to the dog races."

"I'm catching on to it," agreed Rin. "Doesn't seem to be that hard. We just have to sit down while dogs do all the work—chasing an artificial rabbit. Fox hunts should be run the same way with an artificial fox instead of tearing a real fox to pieces at the end of a chase."

"Maybe someday in England, people will go to the fox track," offered Flora.

Then everybody could take part instead of just the richest people," agreed Rin.

"They're about ready for the next race," noted Flora.

Action started with the swiftly moving cloud of heads, bodies, and legs. Gradually the moving form separated into clusters with a few individuals breaking into the lead. They crossed the finish line, resulting in numbers that did not match bets.

The atmosphere of this place is pleasant and southern with warm air, egrets and palms," observed Rin. "Playing the game is fun, although winning would be exciting. Do you win often?"

"Not often," she answered. "But I win more than I lose."

"That's why you come back," he noted.

"Yes," she agreed before enjoying her drink then reviewing trifecta selections for the remaining races.

Rin settled in for the evening and had almost stopped watching numbers on the dogs until a series brought his attention to rechecking numbers he had picked during his second placing of bets. Three dogs in the lead matched his selection although they approached the last turn out of order. Rin felt a twinge of extra excitement as he watched them stretch out pounding toward the finish line and the first two dogs ran almost together. Gripped by anticipation, he could not believe the magic when a photo finish finally flashed the numbers exactly as he had picked them. He checked them and looked again before saying to Flora, "You're not going to believe this but—"

"You didn't," she exclaimed with her blue eyes flashing.

"Yes, I did," he replied.

"Standing up," he asked, "Are you coming?"

"I certainly am," she declared before they hurried to see what had been won.

Of the agent, Rin asked after showing his bet, "Would you please divide that into two equal piles?"

Two piles of cash were prepared then pushed forward. Thanking the agent, Rin gave one to Flora before folding and keeping the other.

"Generous of you," she exclaimed, receiving the cash. "I'll go to the races with you any time."

"We have two more races to watch," he noted before she led the way back to their chairs.

"Seven hundred and fifty dollars," gasped Flora. "A trifecta pays well, depending on the odds."

The next race ran routinely amid continuing excitement from the previous win. The last race alarmed Rin when again he saw his three numbers on lead dogs approaching the last bend. Stretching out at full speed blasting toward the finish, the first two dogs crossed so closely together there was another photo finish. Tensely Rin waited then the results appeared and the first two numbers were in the wrong order. "Almost won that one," he declared. "I had the right selection but just missed with the photo finish."

"Almost twice is spectacular," declared Flora. "All we have to do now is go shopping. There's a mall I would like to visit."

Leaving the building, they walked across a parking lot that vehicles were deserting quickly. Flora gave directions while Rin drove to her favorite mall.

She was soon modeling for him a new bikini. "Looking great," he said admiring her slim and strong form.

"What do you think of this bikini?" she asked, smiling.

"Very good too," he answered.

"I have five I'm checking," she added.

"Why don't you buy them all?" he suggested.

"I'd like to go shopping with him," noted the clerk who waited for Flora's reply.

"Okay—all five," she decided and Rin followed the two women to the sales counter.

Afterward, he bought painting supplies then the two shoppers carried their parcels to the car. During the drive to the resort, Flora said, "Thank you for sharing your winnings."

"Thanks for suggesting the dog races," he replied. "The whole event is interesting. The parts I like the best are the dogs. They live their lives giving all they've got—trying the hardest. They're authentic. That's the way most creatures live. They know all about who they are. They don't have to search for identity or the authentic route to follow. All is known. They just live their lives to the fullest."

"I haven't really thought of it that way," reflected Flora "but the dogs are what attract me. They give all they've got."

"If people could live with such honesty and clarity about what they should be doing, they would know success beyond their wildest expectations," continued Rin. "Yet we spend almost all of our time making decisions about who we are and what we should be doing. The right course is more easily seen by some than by others."

"I've always wanted to be a physiotherapist," offered Flora. "I like to help people heal their injuries or ailments."

"You could not do anything better than to try to help others," observed Rin. "Obviously I don't help people unless they like my paintings."

"Do you prefer painting or photography?" she asked.

"They're much the same," he answered. "For a painting, a worthy topic is selected then the painter has to select all the colors and forms to represent it. With photography, the camera does more of the work combining colors and forms while the photographer concentrates on the selection of subject then presenting it with just the right amount of light."

"Are you going to paint at the beach?" she enquired.

"Yes," he said. "But this is a fishing trip. My girlfriend, Amber Carlson, left me with nothing but advice. She said, 'Go fishing. You might learn something.' Well, maybe she knows me well enough to see that all I needed was that advice. I don't always take advice. However, this time, I listened and here I am."

"We're fishing?" she probed.

"I'm going fishing," he countered. "I'm on the trip now, learning that there's maybe more to fishing than hauling fish out of the water."

"I'm enjoying your fishing trip," offered Flora.

"So am I," he agreed.

They drove quietly the rest of the way and started to get more interested in the journey as they crossed the bridge over the Intracoastal Waterway and then turned northward on the one remaining road.

Seeing the name of the resort where he had booked a room appear in the beam of light from the car, Rin drove onto the parking lot. He and Flora stepped out of the vehicle and approached the office although no light appeared inside. Not surprisingly, the door was locked.

"I forgot to ask if this is like some offices that are always open," affirmed Rin. "We'll have to wait until the place opens in the morning. Likely late to try getting a room anywhere in the area."

"The car is now a motel," concluded Flora.

They drove to a side road and stopped in a clearing with access to the beach. Regular sounds of waves crashing along the sand gave voice to the night. Moonlight glistened on cresting and breaking water.

"This motel has a spectacular view," offered Rin.

"Music's good too," offered Flora.

"Do you want to take the front seat or the back?" asked Rin.

"I'll take the back if you will," she answered while looking directly at him.

"I don't think this is what my ex-girlfriend had in mind when she said, Go fishing. I might learn something," replied Rin, smiling back at her.

"I don't care what your friend thinks," she said before stepping out of the front seat and moving to the back. "I do my own thinking."

After a night in the car with very little sleep, Rin and Flora sat on a sand bank and watched the rising sun bring color and warmth to announce the start of a new dawn. With sunlight dancing on waves the two travelers went for a swim then returned to the office, finding it open. The lady in charge greeted them with a manor revealing years of making people feel at home. She had pale brown eyes and a round face surrounded by sun-bleached, brown hair. "I have you booked in room four," she said, giving Rin a key. "We have other choices if you request a change. Room four faces the Gulf."

"Four sounds great," stated Rin. "Thank you."

They left the office then walked to room four and opened the door. The area was spacious with furniture colored in pastel hues. Pictures on the walls were depictions of beach life. There was a connecting bedroom with two beds along with a side washroom and a kitchenette.

"When we catch fish, we can cook in this room," suggested Rin. "Today though, we'll be visiting restaurants. If you agree, we could leave now for breakfast."

"I hope you always have such good ideas," she declared before they walked to the car.

They drove to a restaurant that appeared to be popular by the number of cars almost filling the parking lot. Inside the building, Rin followed Flora to a table providing a view of the Intracoastal Waterway where boats were tied to docks. At the ends of some docks, there were tall posts topped by cormorants with wings outstretched to welcome warming and drying sunlight.

With an apron covering a stomach that seemed to appear first, a woman approached and said, "Welcome to the best cooking in Florida." Her shape was as abundant as her obvious joy of life. She had black, closely cropped hair and black eyes that shone while apparently looking for something good in any scene. "You both look healthy and happy this morning."

"And tired," added Rin, making Flora laugh.

"Do you need menus?" the woman asked.

"No," answered Flora, followed by Rin.

"I'd like coffee first please," continued Flora, "then scrambled eggs, sausages, toast, and jam—and thank you."

"Lots o' good manners in the ol' restaurant this morning," observed the woman.

"I hope you are always greeted by well-mannered customers," offered Rin.

"I'm sure they would all use them if they all had them," declared the woman. "You have them and this is the way I like to start a day."

When the lady looked directly at Rin and waited with her pad and pencil ready, he said, "Coffee too to start please then pancakes—and thank you."

"On its way," she declared before turning sharply and walking to a counter. She returned to place two full cups on the table in front of Flora and Rin then added, "I'm Sophie Judd."

Indicating his companion, Rin replied, "Flora Chase. I'm Rin Fox. Pleased to meet such a good-natured person—and the coffee's welcome too."

After Sophie had left to place the order, Flora savored some of the stimulating drink while Rin did the same. "Coffee really is the best way to start a day," she declared. "And when are we going fishing?"

"Tomorrow morning," he answered. "Early, break o' dawn, six o'clock."

"That's early and seems even earlier at that time in the morning," stated Flora.

"Give you a chance to see what that time o' day looks like," jabbed Rin.

"I saw it this morning," she countered. "Enjoyed it this morning."

"Fishing trip so far has been fun," said Rin, laughing. "Seems to be more to fishing than hauling fish out o' the water. If the start is any indication, I can get a glimpse of how the world might open up life itself when the prospect of hauling fish out of the water actually occurs."

"I hope I'm there with you to see it," observed Flora.

"We each have a road to walk—our own personal journey no one can take for us just as we can't walk for them," observed Rin. "We are each unique and this makes our journeys original—although there is common ground too because we are all journeying."

The meals arrived and were savored silently. Rin for the first time noticed fishnets hanging from the restaurant's walls where scenes depicted people fishing. Cormorants on posts continued to open their wings to warming sunlight, creating an atmosphere of peacefulness and contentment.

Sophie arrived to leave a bill and refill coffee cups. Following the meal, drinks were sipped slowly. "When we leave here, I could buy a cooler and other supplies to serve you a Margarita on the beach," offered Flora.

"I thought you would never get around to suggesting Margaritas," agreed Rin as he counted out payment for the meal and tip.

"Hope to see you again," said Sophie after Rin and Flora thanked her and started walking away from their table. They left the restaurant, stepping outside into warm, humid air stirred by a breeze from the Gulf. Margarita supplies were purchased on the way back to the resort.

At the beach, pelicans continued to patrol and occasionally dove for fish. Waves crested then crashed ashore, sending water rushing across the sand before returning to move under the next cresting ridge in an unending pattern, as sandpipers chased coquinas and the advancing and returning flows.

"Time for a swim?" asked Rin.

"Yes," she replied before they first wrapped valuables in towels then ran to the water. They dove into the rising side of a curling wave. Greenish, salty water was refreshing and washed away any remnant traces of fatigue.

Sitting down on warm sand, Flora poured Margaritas then gave one to Rin. She also shared sandwiches she had purchased along with other supplies.

Pelicans continued to cross the sky as did the sun. The sunset blazed red tints before these colors faded into night. A colored moon gradually ascended above waves and brought silver light revealing the forms of Flora and Rin who slept on the beach.

At daybreak, they walked to their room to prepare for fishing. When the scheduled time arrived, they drove to the dock, parked the car then met the captain who welcomed them.

"I'm Captain Len Jackson," proclaimed the man who had gray hair dropping to his shoulders to meet a beard of the same color. His nose was curved like an eagle's beak and most noticeable were his eyes that were gray and watery.

"Fishing this morning, we have Flora, actually Florida," explained Rin as he helped her step onto the boat. "I'm Rin—Rinton Fox," he added before getting aboard behind her.

"You can sit down on these benches I've just cleaned," Len directed and we'll get underway.

The boat left the dock, moved slowly along the Intracoastal, cut through a channel then entered the Gulf at what seemed like full speed.

The air was fresh with a salty and fishy fragrance. A broad swath of shore lights narrowed before Len stopped to prepare two lines. He had a thick, dropping mustache that hid his mouth. He groomed these tufts when he appeared to be thinking.

After setting the lines, Len went to the upper deck to operate the boat. He trawled at a steady speed that seemed to match a slow rise and fall of rollers, likely remnants of a distant storm. Other than this movement, the water was almost calm except for a slight ripple caused by a gathering breeze. The water never really rested. Only the morning as a whole seemed calm. The sun started to rise, sending rays of light to glimmer upon the restless sea. Above in a brightening sky, a frigate bird soared. Little else but the water moved.

"I think I'll go and ask the captain if I could operate the boat," said Flora before getting up and proceeding to the higher deck. Their voices added new sounds to the steady drone of the vessel's motor.

While lessons were given on the upper deck, the boat started following a more erratic course and speed varied. Nothing struck the lines.

Something hit Flora's unattended pole. The reel screamed while releasing line. Before Rin could secure his pole to rescue the other, its line broke with a sharp bang then went limp and drifted in the breeze. He reeled in the broken remnant then placed the pole in a corner of the deck.

Rin carefully watched his pole and the line as it slanted out into green rollers topped by dancing sunlight. Gulls and terns flew overhead on a course leading farther out into the Gulf. When the birds started diving to the surface, the vessel turned and moved toward the diving streaks of white.

The boat moved through the area where the birds had been and then came about to cover the same section again. Rin's pole bent into a throbbing half-circle as his reel screamed with the sudden and furious release of line. "Fish on!" he hollered to the upper deck. His call went unheard amid laughter that had been breaking out with increasing frequency. As line continued to scream away from the reel, Rin struggled to the steps then called again, "Fish on!"

"Who cares?" replied Flora.

"I care!" shouted Rin just before the boat started to follow the vanishing line, slowing its release.

Flora's catching something on the upper deck, thought Rin and I've sure caught something huge here on the lower deck. While the vessel followed the fish, line could be retrieved. If approached too closely, the fish retreated to watery depths, swimming away again then slowly returning closer to the surface. This routine continued until the sun was directly above the vessel.

During one of the sequences when the fish was close to the surface, a shark's fin appeared. It broke through the water then circled.

Len came down and said, "That's some monster you've hooked. That'll be the biggest fish this boat has ever caught. You'll be breaking the captain's record." He was grooming his mustache and watching the fin along with the dark form of a shark patrolling the struggles of a great fish.

"You seem to have hooked something yourself," noted Rin, never being one to not say things as he saw them.

There was nothing friendly in the captain's eyes and this was his only reply to the jab. Without speaking he returned to the upper deck. Sounds of voices, broken by occasional laughter resumed, as did the struggle of a hooked fish and surveillance by the shark. Aside from the drone of the boat's motor, the day was quiet until the sun moved from overhead and started taking an afternoon position.

Rin jumped when the Gulf's tranquility was shattered by a steady volley of shots fired by the captain toward the on-looking shark. Bursts of spray covered the form beneath the fin and a stain of blood filled the water.

"Time to get rid of the shark," shouted Len from the upper deck.

"You're not getting rid of a shark," countered Rin. "You're calling all the others. No one catches a bigger fish than the captain."

A cold stare was the captain's reply and Rin knew he had made an enemy.

The boat stopped following the tiring fish closely, allowing it to remain near the surface. Numerous fins started cutting through ripples on the moving sea and a feeding frenzy followed. Churning, spraying water released a wide stain of blood. Rin's line went slack.

He put the pole in a corner next to the other one and then walked to the cooler, opened it, and removed two cans of beer. Sitting on a bench, he drank one beer and then the other before getting up and selecting a third can that he sipped more slowly while the boat sped back toward land.

The captain did not speak to Rin again. There was nothing to say. All was known.

At the dock, the vessel was tied while Rin walked away followed by Flora. They proceeded silently to the car then Flora announced, "I'm going to get my stuff from the trunk."

Rin unlocked it and Flora gathered her things. "Only a bikini is back at the room," she observed. "I guess you know I'm going to stay with Len. I've enjoyed our journey. My destination is with the captain."

"I'm pleased you enjoyed getting here because you're in for some rough sailing," advised Rin.

"I know rough sailing better than the captain," she said with sadness in her eyes. "I've enjoyed your fishing trip."

"I've enjoyed your company," replied Rin, regretting losing her. "You've been a good first mate."

"I think that position has already been taken by Amber Carlson," she said. Trying to end on an upbeat note, she added, "I told you on the plane I'd let you know if I unhook myself. Well, I'm unhooking. Good fishing Rin."

"You're one that got away," he countered. "But I've enjoyed your company."

She turned and walked back toward the boat. When she stepped on board, Rin got into the car and started driving back to the resort.

CHAPTER THREE

WILD SEA

R in settled into the room really for the first time. A particularly comfortable chair provided a view of the Gulf. There was a palmetto, or cabbage, palm just outside the window he planned to keep open most of the time. He liked to hear the leaves, or fronds, rustling in the breeze.

He could not dislodge a feeling of grayness that had settled over him with the loss of Flora. I enjoyed her company, he reflected while sitting in his favorite chair and trying to see a new path to walk or a way to proceed. She connected naturally with the captain, but I wonder if she knows what he did to get rid of the fish I might have caught that would have outshone his previous record. I tried to warn her. She was confident she could navigate through rough times. Apparently, she had already experienced them. I don't think that's a good reason for returning to them.

Sipping some more cold coffee that he had purchased on the way back from the day's fishing, he concluded, I was told to go fishing because I might learn something. Well, then, I should buy equipment for the rest of my journey, I'll be my own captain.

He left the chair, stepped out of the room then locked the door, and proceeded to his car. He drove to a well-supplied store and bought fishing equipment along with frozen shrimp for bait. Lastly, he stopped at a restaurant for a meal.

Rin selected a beach oyster bar he had enjoyed previously with Flora. Maybe it would bring sunshine to dispel the cloud left by his recent attempt at fishing. The server again was Sophie Judd, a woman of sturdy build along with a no-nonsense attitude, and likely behind this gruff exterior, there was a very kind person.

"How can I cheer you up today?" she enquired.

"Are you psychic or is my gray mood that obvious?" he asked.

"Both," she answered, sizing people up quickly and knowing she liked this guy with strong, well-chiseled facial features, brown eyes, and gray hair. The tan he is acquiring suits him, she concluded.

"To get into the mood of this region, I would like to try fried oysters, clam chowder, and a grouper sandwich with cheese accompanied by your choice of draft beer," he outlined.

"That combo should kill or cure," she stated while making notes on a pad she had pulled from a frayed apron.

"Are you the cook too?" he asked.

"Yes, along with most everything else," she explained with black eyes flashing.

"You seem like an in-charge kind o' person," observed Rin.

"If you want me to take charge o' you and cure what ails you, I recommend my key lime pie," she declared. "This is my cure and for a cure today there's no charge. I make the best key lime pie in all of Florida."

"Thank you," he exclaimed. "Please add your most appreciated cure to the rest of the meal. Maybe the cure should come first."

"No," she declared. "After the meal, you'll really need a cure—and I'm only joking."

"The doctor knows best," replied Rin.

"Smart person," she said. "You'll do well around here." She proceeded to the bar, poured a tall glass of draft. After placing the drink in front of Rin, she walked to the kitchen.

Having enjoyed some draft, Rin thought, maybe this place is a beacon guiding me to a better part of my fishing trip.

When the meal arrived, it was delicious. The key lime pie was thick and filled with the finest, most refreshing flavor, seeming to represent the best of all the tastes of Florida.

The bill arrived and Rin said to Sophie, "Your cure was a slice of Florida—that was better than anything else."

"If you come back," she replied, "I'll give you my other cure—the first time—for no charge."

"If it's anything like the first, the second will be greatly appreciated," replied Rin.

"Hope to see you soon," she concluded before walking away to meet other arriving customers.

Rin left payment at the table to cover the bill plus a large tip. He drove back to his room at the resort where he added line to the new reel and pole before attaching a hook and sinker.

Carrying his fishing pole along with a bucket, to contain any fish he might catch, he left the resort and walked to the water's edge. He baited the hook with a shrimp then swung the pole back before sending it forward in what was expected to be a cast that would hurl the bait far out over the water. The line started to release, as expected, then unraveled from the reel in a tangled knot. The baited hook started a beautifully arcing journey toward the Gulf until the knotted line ended all progress so suddenly the hooked shrimp not only stopped but shot back almost hitting Rin as it whizzed past his head.

He gathered his equipment and as the fishing trip ended so did the day. The setting sun drew to itself hues of pink, red then purple before vanishing beyond a clouded horizon withdrawing most color from the sky.

Back at his room, he found the line to be in such a tangle it had to be cut away from the reel. He drove to the supply store and bought some new line. Upon request, he also received much advice on using his equipment. He was also shown how to apply a cast net he was told to purchase in order to catch minnows for bait.

Returning to the resort, he reassembled his tackle then practiced on the lawn in front of the room. He was weary by the time he felt he had mastered the arts of sending out a line and also a net.

He slept soundly that night and welcomed morning for the promise it held of a new beginning. He drove to a restaurant specializing in breakfast where he started the rest of his fishing trip by ordering coffee and pancakes.

"So what brings you to these shores?" asked the server after she placed a cup of coffee on the table in front of him.

"I was told to go fishing because I might learn something," he answered.

"So you're going fishing?" she asked. Blondish hair was combed away from her fresh, young face where her greenish eyes sparkled.

"Yes," he replied.

"And you have learned something?" she enquired again, smiling.

"So far I probably have become basically proficient at using a fishing pole and a cast net," he confirmed.

"You seem to be starting a great journey," she added exuberantly. "My uncle says anyone can go fishing but most fish are caught by very few fishermen."

"Sounds like I just learned something important this morning," he noted, reaching for the coffee cup.

"Always pleased to help a traveler on his journey," she declared before walking away, leaving Rin with coffee to help begin the remainder of his quest. There's more to fishing than I thought, he concluded.

The pancakes arrived and they were savored before being followed by more coffee. Rin paid his bill along with including a large tip then left the restaurant and walked into the sunshine and the promise of a new day.

Back at the resort, he wasted no time in assembling tackle. The warming sun soon found him sitting on a chair located on the sand at the water's edge. He held his fishing pole as it bent slightly while the taut line stretched out into greenish-blue water. Slight waves splashed along the shore in a repetitive rhythm, establishing a peaceful atmosphere, one of the best moods of the restless Gulf. These same waters, he mused, with the right winds, can become anything but peaceful and turn into a raging and almost unstoppable force.

Startling Rin, his rod bent and throbbed when something took the bait. Line tore from the reel. Trembling with excitement, he tried to control the rush. By tightening the tension, he started to regain line, bringing the fighter gradually toward shore.

Finally able to pull the fish up to the sand, Rin realized from his fishing notes he had caught a catfish—a gafftopsail catfish or sail cat. He picked up his catch, finding it to be large, maybe about three pounds.

The creature swung its front half rapidly from side to side, sending a prong in a fin through Rin's index finger from the front end almost through to the knuckle. Severe pain increased as the fish continued to thrash from side to side. Blood sprayed from the wound with each thrust.

Calling to a nearby fisherman, Rin held up the fish and shouted, "Hey! Do you have pliers?"

The man checked his equipment, seemed to have found piers then ran to help. "I got speared by one o' these things too," he said as he positioned a cutting edge on the barb, snapped it, and released the fish, dropping it back into the water.

"Thank you," exclaimed Rin. "That shaft is extremely painful and the critter kept twisting, sending the barb in farther."

"A walk-in clinic can't help you with that," explained the guy. "I went to one with the same wound. They just told me I had to go straight to the hospital."

"Thank you for all your help," repeated Rin. He liked this helpful guy who was tall, lean with a weather-toughened face that portrayed a hard-working person who had led an honorable life, leading to riches in ways not involving money. Silvery-gray hair also spoke of years gathering knowledge. His clothes were particularly clean and his eyes were blue.

The helper returned to fishing while Rin quickly drove to a hospital where he was met with as many jokes as notes of sympathy. The doctor was a tall, lean swarthy individual who was well-tanned from an obviously outdoor lifestyle. "I've had to remove a lot o' these barbs," he noted. "They'll go through boots and even into bones." He moved the shaft, enlarging the opening sufficiently to remove the object that was serrated to keep it from being easily dislodged. After applying a tetanus shot, he said, "You are free to fish again. Maybe next time you can catch the fish."

"There's more to fishing than I thought," acknowledged Rin. "Thank you for your help. I'll try to remember your advice—I'm supposed to catch the fish."

"The tetanus shot will protect you from your next incident," explained the doctor.

"There are more to come?" asked Rin with exaggerated alarm.

"Life causes injuries," said the doctor. "That's why I went in for medicine. I knew I'd be needed."

"You certainly are," agreed Rin. "I'm not sure where I'm needed."

"That's a road of discovery we're all here to walk," added the doctor.

"I'm grateful for your work," noted Rin before the doctor moved on to other patients. Rin walked to his car and drove back to his room.

Sitting on the sand in front of the resort, he watched the sun gather to itself colors from the sky before descending, leaving behind afterglow in growing darkness. Amber Carlson told me to go fishing, he recalled. She said I might learn something. I have started fishing and I am learning. There's a lot more to fishing than I thought.

The next morning, the first rays of sunlight brightening the dawn outlined Rin as he sat on a chair at the water's edge. He watched the day awaken. Pelicans swooped in, taking their positions just above the water where sunlight danced on slight swells moving toward shore. Sandpipers hunted coquinas. The world seemed crisp, fresh, and new, starting over again with a memory of the past and a promise of the future, but only the separate daily segments mattered.

Rin's pole bent wildly as something tore line from his screaming reel. Fortunately, the first rush lessened then settled into a steady struggle.

Seem to have something good on now, thought Rin while he started being able to reel in line. Excitement gave way to disappointment when into shallows by the shore he pulled a stingray. To release this creature, he stepped into the water, moved his hand along the taut line toward the hook. He was trying to work the hook free when a searing pain shot through his foot. The ray has speared the end of its tail into the top of my foot, he decided just as the hook became dislodged and in a swirl, the stingray swam toward deeper blue water.

With his foot feeling like it was on fire, he assembled his equipment then awkwardly walked toward his room. The manager was greeting the morning as she often did by sitting on a chair in front of her resort. Sipping coffee while watching the day begin, she saw what had happened, and at Rin's approach, she enquired, "Speared by a stingray?"

"Yes," he answered. "I thought when I went fishing, I was supposed to catch the fish. So far, they've been catching me."

"They only catch strangers," she advised. "You'll have to get to know them. For now, you'll need a tetanus shot then soak your foot in soapy water as hot as you can stand it. I'll bring you some medicine to drink."

"I've been unlucky by getting injured, but lucky to have helpers coming to the rescue," he replied.

"Welcome to life by the sea," she exclaimed. "You soak your foot. I'll mix something to help. My name is Florence, but I'm usually known as Flo."

Paying closer attention to her, Rin noticed that everything about her spoke of strength. Her largeness was in no way soft. Her sun-bleached brown hair was cut short to be functional rather than attractive in line with her practical approach to life.

Rin was soaking his foot when Flo presented him with a tall glass of beer. "You and that medicine are both a welcome sight," he declared. "The drink is very soothing. Is it spiked?"

"Yes," she answered. "It's part of my standard remedy. You're not the first one to get speared by a sting ray."

"I've already had a tetanus shot," he noted.

"Good," she confirmed. "You need it. In the future, pull the ray up on shore then use something like the legs of a chair to flip the thing over on its back. This immobilizes the critter and prevents the spear from working. After unhooking, use the chair again to turn the ray over and push it back into the water."

"I was told to learn something on this trip. I've been learning—but always the hard way," he explained.

"That's my way too," she replied before gazing into the distance as if seeing her past. People who have an easy life seem to know what to do and proceed to success without walking down the roads that should not be taken. People like you and I tend to see what not to do by getting bitten by it. After each bite, we see the road to take."

"So far on this fishing trip, I've learned what not to do without discovering what I should be doing," admitted Rin.

"Keep trying," she advised. "You'll find your way." Walking toward the doorway, she added, "You'll be okay now. I have coffee calling me."

"You're a good doctor," Rin said appreciatively.

"Experience is what I've got about the world of fish—and this is what you're getting," she added before leaving.

"Thanks, Flo" he shouted while she returned to her chair.

Gradually pain left Rin's foot enabling him to resume searching for some kind of order. Life that is based on the sea seems to have a routine, and I'd like to find a place in it, he mused while driving to a restaurant, the same oyster bar he had previously visited.

After he sat down at his usual table, Sophie approached with a flare of the take-charge manner. "What medicine can the good doctor give you today," she asked.

"Could we start with a bowl of fish chowder and then a grouper sandwich with cheese?" he answered.

"Got it," she stated and walked away, returning quickly with a cup of coffee.

"Thank you," he said. "I forgot to mention this."

"Sometimes we overlook the most important things in life while busying ourselves with the unimportant." She declared.

"Is there an extra charge for the philosophy?" he asked.

"No," she declared, smiling. "I dispense that—or inflict that—for free."

"Good thing there's no charge because the philosophy sounds valuable and would be very expensive," he added.

"The best things in life are free," she exclaimed.

After leaving the restaurant, Rin drove back to the resort and noticed he had missed a deluge of rain. Water that had pooled on the parking lot continued to drip from foliage and flowed along drainage ditches. Southern climate brings heavy downpours although they often don't last, observed Rin after parking his car and starting to walk to his room. Lizards scampered off sidewalks as he approached. Maybe there's a rainbow at the end of each downpour, he reflected while he noticed a woman checking into room eight. *She reminds me of Amber Carlson with her black hair and eyes. She's also tall and slim. This woman's hair though is long. Always helps to have good neighbors.* He waved to her but she pretended not to notice. *She's aloof but likely that's a good sign,* he concluded before entering his room.

He sat in his favorite chair providing a view of the beach. *Sun is setting,* he noted. *Large waves are breaking along the shore. Must've been a greater storm farther out in the Gulf as the wind has strengthened also.*

The next morning, he greeted the new day by again sitting in his chair and checking the outside world. He noted that large waves continued to crash against the sand. *Won't be any fishing today,* he concluded. *Maybe I'll start with the breakfast restaurant then go for a long walk along the beach.*

A cardinal sang from a long leaf pine draped with Spanish moss when Rin left his car in the lot then walked to the restaurant. He sat at the same table he had selected previously and was again approached by the woman with blondish hair, fresh young face, and green-tinted eyes.

"You're back," she said before placing a cup of coffee on his table.

"Good to see you again," he replied. "Do you work here all the time?"

"Just in the mornings," she answered. "I'm a student the rest o' the day and night. "I'm going to be a vet. Along with regular work, I help at the bird sanctuary. We have to look after the Gulf's health along with all wildlife, particularly fish. People depend on them for food. Without minnows, there would be few fish. Many creatures of the Gulf rely on minnows to the same extent wildlife on land rely on small game such as gophers out west. People overlook the vital importance of minnows and gophers.

I'm Jack, actually Jacquelyn Pearce."

"Pleased to meet you," he said. "I'm Rin Fox. The world is a better place because you're in it."

"Wow," she exclaimed. "That gets the morning off to a good start. Pancakes again?"

"Yes—and grits," he answered.

Jack left to place the order, leaving Rin with the hot drink to stir his thoughts. I've always thought people like Jack are lucky, he reflected, because they know what they want to do and where they are going. They don't wander—lost—wondering what they should be doing, the way I have struggled most of my life. Presently I've been trying to be a fisherman and so far have failed with every attempt. Again I wonder if I should be walking a different path. I was told to go fishing because I might learn something but maybe this entire adventure is a mistake. I seem to be lost. Jack knows where she's going and how to get there."

The pancakes arrived along with grits. While savoring his breakfast, Rin looked through windows to the beach where large waves continued to crash along the sand.

When the bill arrived, he paid it in addition to leaving the usual large tip. He stepped outside into a brisk wind laced with a slightly salty and fishy fragrance.

He returned to the resort where he parked his car then started walking along the shore. The water was churned and murky. Strands of dislodged vegetation were deposited by waves crashing against the sand.

I certainly won't be fishing until the water settles, he concluded as he commenced a fast-paced stride that sent him past estate-style houses back from the water. A coast guard vessel was tossed wildly by waves as the craft passed slowly offshore. Rather than disturb the birds, he walked around flocks of gulls and terns resting on the sand and facing the wind.

He could taste salt from the wind as he walked, enjoying the feeling of joining the motion of life around him. He felt exalted by becoming part of the pace of life. Everything seemed to be moving. Palms back from the sand were swaying. Clouds drifted high above the wildness of the sea.

Getting tired, he walked to a bar and crab shack surrounded by swaying palms. Inside, there was a spacious, bright room where light entered from numerous windows providing a view of the Gulf. Most of this open area was filled with tables and chairs. A bar with seats beside it ran along one side.

Sitting at the bar, Rin ordered a small dish of fried oysters along with draft beer.

"Did you just blow in or did you come here on purpose?" asked a congenial bartender who had a reddish complexion along with brown, curly hair. The glasses he wore added a glint to black eyes. He was overweight, having pudgy cheeks, and a protruding stomach that a short-sleeved shirt struggled to cover. He appeared to be a person who liked to talk, making him many people's choice for a bartender. A tattoo of a bikini clad beach beauty covered much of his thick arm.

Rin couldn't help but notice the tattoo. When he was caught looking at it, the bartender said, "It's like the song Margaritaville when Jimmy Buffett sings about going on a holiday and having nothing to show for it but a tattoo and he doesn't know how he got it. Well, that's how I got this. It's a constant reminder for me to adopt a more moderate lifestyle."

"Whoever gave you the tattoo did you a favor," said Rin.

"Yes," he replied. "I'd have preferred him or her to just tell me the advice—but then likely I would not have listened."

"The harder lessons do seem to get our attention," agreed Rin. "I always learn things the hard way. I've been trying to go fishing. So far my girlfriend left to stay with a boat captain, I've been speared by a sail cat and also a stingray—and I'm just getting started."

"With that record," exclaimed the guy, "imagine how knowledgeable you'll be by the time you master the art of fishing. We all have a calling. Lucky ones hear it and others don't. I heard my calling when I first started dealing with people. That's how I see the world—from the point o' view of a bartender. Just when I think I've seen it all, another outstandingly unique individual will arrive and give me an entirely new view of life. Therefore, my work is endlessly interesting—although, just like fishing, it's sometimes dangerous. That's enough about me. I'm Reg Wills—at your service."

"I haven't been successful at fishing but the people around that world have been interesting and you are definitely one of them," said Rin. "Pleased to meet you. I'm Rin Fox."

"Well Mr. Fox would you care for another draft," he asked.

"Thought you'd never ask," replied Rin. A tall glass of draft arrived quickly. The outer surface of the glass was damp with beads of moisture. "Thank you," said Rin. "Nothing like a really cold beer on a very warm day."

"Yes," agreed Reg. "And there's no extra charge for all the chatter you have to wade through in order to get a beer."

"Chatter's the best part o' this place—although other parts are good too," stated Rin.

"Well, thank you," exclaimed Reg.

"My chatter can get blunt sometimes and people get offended," noted Reg.

"I've never found getting well informed to be offensive," added Rin.

"Good to hear it," said Reg.

"Now that I've met an interesting person, been fortified by some fine oysters and beer, I'm ready to walk back into the world," concluded Rin. "What are the damages?"

After paying the bill, he thanked Reg then stepped out into salty wind. I don't really know where I'm going, he declared to himself, but I'm enjoying my journey trying to get there.

He walked back to the room. Sleep came easily and morning sunshine found him sitting on his chair at the beach and watching line slanting out into the water.

Pelicans, almost always in small groups and seeming to be a permanent part of the water, flew effortlessly past, skimming above waves. Occasionally, with wings folded in place, one or all in the group would dive then return to the surface to raise their heads and swallow the catch. Seagulls would occasionally land on a pelican's head and steal a fish.

Porpoises surfaced to get air before submerging again to continue hunting for fish. Most creatures, including myself, are after fish for food, reflected Rin; yet very few people are aware of the need to protect minnows. The sea is alive, he thought, after a manatee swam past close to shore.

Rin watched in awe when surface water bent upwards as it was displaced and sent over the backs of a large school of fish, swimming a short distance out from shore. They were likely jacks, determined Rin as he checked regulations and charts identifying different types of fish found in this part of the Gulf.

Something large hit Rin's bait and bent the pole in a half-circle. He jumped to his feet and could only watch while the line shot out from the screaming reel. A lot of line had been released before the action stopped just as suddenly as it had started. Rin pulled back on the pole yet no response followed. Line could not be retrieved nor was any more released. Nothing moved except the other fisherman on the beach. He approached and soon Rin recognized the same person who had cut the barb to remove the catfish.

"At least you're getting action," said the fisherman calmly as if nothing about fishing could any longer surprise him. "Looks like you hooked a large ray. It has stopped swimming and just buried itself in the sand. I suggest you pull hard on the line. You'll either dislodge the ray or most likely the line will break."

Rin did as recommended. A sharp bang split the air as the line snapped. A section curled back through the air then settled in the water. "That's better than bringing in a large ray," concluded Rin.

"Yes," agreed the fisherman.

"Thanks again for your help cutting the catfish off my finger," said Rin.

"You're getting experience," noted the fisherman.

"Maybe someday I'll catch a good fish," offered Rin. "I'm Rin Fox— and as you can see I have a lot to learn about fishing."

"I'm Cory Woods," replied the fisherman. "There's a lot more to fishing than people think. More is involved than baiting a hook and throwing out a line. That much anyone can do. But real fishing is an art. It must be carried out with respect not only for fish but also for the world where they live. I've worked at different jobs in factories all my life. Likely that's why I aspire to be outside. There's something about the shore that's most attractive. Although buildings might fill the backdrop, there's no taming the wilderness of the sea. I've made my share of mistakes. One time in Maui I was swimming then stood up and turned my back on the water for too long. I heard a hissing sound behind and above me. On turning around, I saw a green wall of water cresting at the top and showing white spray against a blue sky. Then the swell hit. I was tumbled under churning water. I put my arms and hands out to protect my face from being slammed against lava rocks at the bottom. Then I got tossed up onto the steeply sloping beach. The backwash of water returning to the sea carried me under the next swell and I got tossed up again. This time I managed to dig my heels into the sand and resist getting carried back to the ocean. When you're in Hawaii—or anywhere—watch the water."

"Fortunately swells don't come in here like that," exclaimed Rin.

"No," he agreed. "But water's always moving and if people don't destroy it, the sea will continue to teem with life. It's unendingly interesting."

"Thanks for sharing your stories," observed Rin.

"My wife says I talk too much—but never at the right times," added Cory, smiling, revealing particularly white teeth.

"When you have a story to tell, I'll always have time to listen," stated Rin.

"Or you could just pick up your chair and leave," joked Cory.

"I've almost made nothing but mistakes on this trip but that won't be one of them," affirmed Rin.

"I'd better see what else is biting," said Cory before he started walking back toward his chair and equipment.

Rin fished until the sun stood overhead. The heat of the day seemed to be a good time to move to the shade provided by palms.

He carried his equipment to his room then, in a short time, stepped outside again. He took a can of beer to one of a group of chairs located in the shade provided by palms. This location also offered a fine view of the beach and caught much of an almost constantly stirring breeze.

Resting on the chair, he sipped the refreshing drink while he watched a frigate bird hover among a few clouds drifting far above the water. Backs of porpoises broke through the surface while these graceful swimmers moved past on one of their routine journeys along the shoreline.

The slim woman with long, black hair left room eight. She carried a towel and walked toward the water. Leaving the towel on the sand, she waded out, and moving as gracefully as a porpoise, her back slipped beneath the surface. She reappeared farther out amid bluish-green water.

She isn't friendly, noted Rin, but she's the most beautiful part of this scene. The woman returned to the shore, used the towel to get dry then walked back to her room.

A short time later, the blue sky in front of Rin was filled with a can of beer held by the woman. She had approached from behind and he had not seen her.

Accepting the beer, he said, "Thank you. I've seen a lot of things in a blue sky, but that's the first time a can o' beer has appeared."

She sat down on an adjacent chair, opened a second can, sipped the drink then sat back to look at the view. "I was wondering," she said, "if you would accompany me to my favorite bar."

"I thought you'd never ask," he replied.

"I thought you'd never ask," she countered.

"I like to give people their space and not intrude on them," he explained.

"That's why I like you and decided to ask you out this evening," she replied.

"Usually my lack of pushing forward gets me farther behind not farther ahead," he added.

"I don't like pushy, aggressive men," she stated with her eyes flashing.

"You talk from experience and I can see why you would get experience," observed Rin.

"Thank you," she said, smiling for the first time. "You aren't even aggressive with your compliments."

"I'm one of the few people who are perfect," he joked, "and you're the only other one I've met."

"Thank you again," she replied.

Talk came easily and seemed to fit with all the other beautiful aspects of the day as the sun crossed the sky and started painting the Gulf and clouds with crimson hues. A flock of egrets appeared to be particularly white in contrast to a background of darkening colors.

The woman stood up, outstretched her hand, and said "I'm Corina Sims."

Standing, Rin shook hands and said, "Rin—Rinton Fox. Really pleased to meet you."

"Meet you in the parking lot in an hour?" she asked.

"Thank you," he replied before they walked to their rooms.

Rin showered, changed clothes, and was waiting by his car when Corina arrived. She walked to her car and waited until he approached. She got in the driver's side then started the motor before Rin sat on the passenger's side.

She drove quickly although not carelessly and parked on the lot of an oyster bar. "This is your favorite bar?" he asked as they left the vehicle and started walking toward the main entrance.

"I know it's supposed to be a popular place," she said. He glanced at her and was struck by her beauty. The night was warm and starlit with a slight breeze stirring from the Gulf. Palm leaves could be heard rustling.

Noticing his look, she asked, "What?"

"Nothing," he answered.

She stopped and watched him.

"Let's go in," he suggested.

She waited until he said, "It's too obvious to mention."

"Making a lot over a small thing maybe, but I like to hear it," she explained.

"While walking, during this warm night, with stars above and palm leaves rustling, I noticed, of it all, you were the most beautiful part," he explained.

She remained quiet for a while then said, "Let's go in."

They entered the building, finding it to be moderately busy. Corina led the way past the bar and selected a table providing a view through open windows to the beach. "Okay?" she asked.

He nodded and they sat down facing each other. A woman server approached. Her eyes were dark blue, hair short and brown. She flashed a bright, friendly smile while supplying menus.

Glancing at the choices, Corina said, "Red snapper dinner with rice—and a Margarita."

Turning to Rin, the server asked, "and you?"

"The same dinner with draft beer," he answered.

"Okay," she replied. "Be right back." She walked away and soon returned with the drinks, placing them on the table in front of Corina and Rin.

"Thank you," noted Corina. The woman left and walked to meet other customers.

After taking a long sample of the Margarita, Corina said, "So you're a fisherman."

"Not yet," he replied. "Right now I'm just trying to be one."

"And why are you trying to be one," she enquired.

"When my girlfriend left," he explained, "all she left me with was some advice. She said, 'Go fishing. You might learn something.'"

"Wonder why she would leave you?" enquired Corina.

"She was annoyed because she thought I didn't know who I was," he explained. "Maybe she knew but I didn't."

"So you are on a quest," she observed. "You're fishing for you."

"Insightful way of putting it," he mused. "What brought you to room eight?"

"My boyfriend—partner—left one day and just didn't come back. I kept waiting, yet he did not return. So I left. Decided I could use a holiday and that's how I came to be in room eight."

Dinner arrived and so did the band. Loud music brought people to the dance floor. The music—or noise with a beat—took over the place.

Following the meal along with two more drinks, Corina came to the part Rin wanted to avoid when she asked, "Do you want to dance?"

"I can't dance," he stated directly.

"That's what I thought you were going to say," she said. She rested until a slow song started then stood up and waited. He walked with her to the dance floor. They started to dance. Struck again by her attractiveness, he was forgetting his inability to dance when a guy barged in between them saying, "My turn."

He grabbed Corina and started dancing but she slammed her fist against his mouth, jolting his bead back. He stopped, put one hand up to his lips. His fingers reddened with blood. He punched Corina on the side of her face, knocking her backward.

Rin stepped forward, slugged the aggressor first with a right then a left fist. The guy kept standing yet was dazed. Rin picked him up, walked him a short distance then tossed him over the bar. As he fell, one of his legs hit a back wall, causing an explosion of falling shelves and breaking bottles.

Rin ran to the server, gave her some bills, and said, "This is for dinner and the rest is for you."

He returned to Corina and they both rushed toward the door. A bouncer grabbed Rin and slammed a fist against the side of his head. Rin went down but came back quickly just in time to see Corina's foot bury itself in the guy's crotch. Holding his fly, he fell forward gasping.

Rin and Corina left the building and ran to the car. Quickly they were inside. With tires squealing, the vehicle swerved around a corner of the lot before entering the street. Reducing speed, she drove back to the resort.

"Come inside," she said. "I'll check your injuries."

"How are you?" he asked while they walked to her room.

"Sore but nothing's broken," she replied while unlocking the door.

Inside the room, Rin sat down while Corina dampened towels then brought one over to Rin. He applied it to his face while Coring did the same with her bruise.

"Your beauty draws attention," he noted. "Thank you for your help. I must remember to never make you angry."

Laughing, she said, "Thank you for your help. How do you feel?"

"I'll likely survive," he replied, smiling, sending an extra bolt of pain through his jaw. "How are you?"

"A little achy," she explained. "But actually I had a great time. I'm going to celebrate. We are going to celebrate," she added before turning off the lights. He could not believe his sudden good luck as he was swept into paradise.

When Rin woke up the next morning, he had a headache. He left Corina's side, walked to his room, and then allowed sleep to come. He awoke occasionally until night's shadows were replaced by morning sunlight.

When there was a knock at the door, he got up slowly, opened it, and was pleased to see Corina. She brought in packages and said, "I have breakfast—coffee, grits, and pancakes."

"You couldn't get better than you are," he exclaimed.

"I had breakfast at the restaurant," she noted while opening one of two large cups of coffee. "These things are for you."

She sipped the drink and Rin enjoyed the food. "Considerate of you," he said after finishing the meal and starting on coffee.

"I appreciate your help at the bar," she said. "I didn't know bar room thugs could fly."

"He should not have hit you," affirmed Rin. "I appreciate your help too. I didn't know bar room bouncers had trouble with their crotches," he added starting more laughter.

"Something has happened," she said with a serious tone in her voice.

"Oh, oh," he replied.

"My partner has returned," she continued. "He said he didn't leave. He's just late getting back. He went to a party, got involved with drugs, and was delayed. He says he is not going to let it happen again."

"If your world is the way you want it then that's the way it'll be," he stated as carefully as possible although he was shocked and disappointed. "I've always determined that I can't cry about what I don't have but will work with what I've got. I'll miss you."

"I'll miss you too," she countered. Silence followed until she said, "I should go. He's in the room. I told him I was with you at the bar last night and you got injured helping me. I was going to get your breakfast."

"We must enjoy—make the best of—the moment, and we did because we never know how long each occasion will last," he said.

"And value is not determined by length of time," she added. "I'll look forward to seeing you again."

"And I'll look for you," he said before she walked to the door, opened it, and without looking back walked away.

Rin was hit by a feeling of loss. It increased his other pain. He tried to sleep yet it too seemed to have left and he could not get it back.

Knowing only time would lessen a gray mood that had settled over him, he left the room, walked to the beach, and started following the shore. Gulls cried and swarmed above minnows splashing at the surface where they must've been driven by fish below. Pelicans and terns dove into the same school. Above in a pale blue sky, a frigate bird soared. This clamor of life remained distant, blocked by a gray cloud that seemed to be following Rin. Grayness diminished partially after one mile of the beach had moved past then had almost lifted by the time the crab shack came into view.

Entering the building, Rin was greeted by the bartender, Reg Wills who smiled, stretched out his arms, and asked, "Dumped again?"

"Yes," came the answer while Rin sat on a chair beside the bar.

"That's twice?" he asked again, smiling.

"Three times actually," Rin replied. "And in a short time."

"Well, let's look at the bright side," said Reg with his already reddish complexion brightening, "You must be a really dumpable kind of guy," and they both laughed.

"Well, thanks for that," said Rin. "You sure know how to cheer a guy up."

"That's me," he affirmed. "Here to help."

"Could you help with a daft and a burger?" he asked.

"I'll place the order," replied Reg. "Would you like our high in fat beach favorite or our no fat veggie burger?"

"Let's try the veggie burger," he answered.

"Coming right up," Reg affirmed. "People are wanting healthier food all the time. Even I've caught on to it."

After placing the order and bringing Rin a glass of draft, Reg waited until his customer had sampled the drink before saying, "I don't just serve food and drink here. I also have advice. What other things were you doing before you started this fishing trip?"

"Office manager, painter, and photographer," he outlined.

"There's your solution," Reg exclaimed. "Take a break. Do some painting for a while. It ties in with a fishing trip. You can paint other people fishing along with the Gulf and shore."

"Now we're getting somewhere," Rin stated, knowing he had heard the right idea at the right time. "Now I see why you are successful. You go the extra mile."

"I enjoy my work," Reg added. "It's more than food and drink. Every problem has a solution if we can see it."

The veggie burger arrived and, after sampling it, Rin stated, "Amazing how delicious healthy food is."

"Tastes are acquired," offered Reg. "We can change them."

Rin enjoyed the burger and a second glass of draft. Before leaving the bar he said to Reg, "Thank you for helping me to see the better way."

Outside the building, he stepped into a refreshing breeze coming off the Gulf. My gray mood has lifted, he thought before he started walking back to the resort. He quickly returned to a fast pace, again finding the beach to be interesting.

He walked around a group of ibises, not wanting to disturb them. Gulls cried and circled overhead while pelicans as usual patrolled the water.

Returning to his room, he assembled the painting supplies purchased with dog track winnings. Feeling a new optimism, he walked to the beach, set up an easel, and placed a board on it before placing a chair and surrounding it with paints and related supplies.

As was his custom, he quickly covered the board, painting in sky, sand, and water. Afterward, he tried to summon the realm of creativity whereby he attempted to match colors of the Gulf to hues and shades he applied to his picture. He tried and struggled again yet a match would not come. Amazing color combinations of sand, water, and sky escaped being captured and represented by applications of paint. Each time he wiped away one attempt at a picture and started another he cleared it also.

I'm just out of practice, he told himself. However, further attempts the next day then a third convinced him to put away his materials and go for a walk.

He quickly established his fast stride and, in what seemed like a short time, he entered the crab shack.

"Not dumped again?" shouted Reg from behind the bar.

"Yes," stated Rin before returning to his customary chair. "And this time by a paintbrush."

"Oh, oh," gasped Reg. "This is serious. The first draft is on the house." After serving the beer, he noted, "We got a fresh batch o' crabs in if you're interested."

"Thanks," said Rin, "but maybe I could just stay with some fried oysters and clam chowder."

"Coming right up," confirmed Reg before he placed the order through a window opening to the kitchen.

The food came quickly and it brought to Rin a slight return of contentment. "I like your establishment here," he noted when Reg brought a second glass of draft. "Your place is bright and cheerful—as is the bartender."

"Well, thank you," the reddish-complexioned man replied.

"I started thinking though, while walking in here, continued Rin, that I should maybe quit and go home."

"Oh, oh," gasped Reg. "Beer is on the house today—so is the food. I know a lot about quitters and losers because I get a lot o' them in here. And I can tell you—from an authority—you're not one of them."

"That's what I needed," stated Rin before he finished the second draft. He removed from his pocket a large bill. Slapping it down on the counter, he declared, "Food and drinks are on the house so that's a tip— and thank you."

He stood up, strode to the door, and was stepping outside when he heard Reg exclaim, "Wow!"

Walking back to the resort, Rin thought, I haven't been successful so far on this fishing trip but at least I'm certain I'll keep trying. I'm not just persevering because Amber told me to go fishing. I'm undertaking this journey because I've always known she was right.

Back at the resort, he assembled his fishing equipment then walked to the beach. After placing his chair on the sand, he picked up his cast net and waded into shallows where he had seen minnows splashing at the surface. Holding the net's upper section with his right hand, he let the weighted ends fall before using his left hand to gather some ends he brought up to his right hand. Next, he tossed the open circle of weights out and up. The edges of the circle dropped into the water, trapping minnows. Weights closed together when the net was pulled to shore to be emptied, tumbling minnows into the bait bucket.

After hooking a minnow, Rin moved back the end of his pole before swinging it forward, sending the bait out to deep water. The minnow had hardly settled before the pole bent and throbbed sharply as it responded to struggles of a large fish.

Following the initial shock of the bite, the battle settled into a routine of line first screaming out from the reel then being rewound. While keeping the line taut, Rin noticed the person who had been fishing farther down the beach had left his equipment and was coming to watch the action. When he approached, Rin was pleased to see that the other person was Cory Woods.

"You've got something big," noted Cory.

"Hope it's something good," replied Rin.

"The sharp pulls indicate it might be a shark," suggested Cory. "You have to watch them. They're one of the few—maybe only—fish that will try to bite you."

As line was rewound, a dark, streamlined form moved out of deeper bluish water and Cory confirmed, "It's a shark."

Rin pulled the struggling fish up onto the sand. He held the fish with his left hand then reached out with his right to remove the hook.

Jaws snapped at the approaching hand. Rin responded instantly, pulling his hand clear although the jaws were able to clamp onto his thumb, hitting the center of the nail. The pain increased when the head tried to thrash from side to side in a tearing movement. Rin countered these efforts as much as possible, using his left hand to subdue the creature. No effort would loosen the jaws.

"Only one way to solve this," stated Cory as he snapped open a filleting knife. A few skillful thrusts severed the shark's head then Cory pulled open the jaws, releasing the thumb.

"Wow," shouted Rin. "I was in a rough place there. You saved me from an iron grip."

"Sharks will attack," affirmed Cory. "Maybe that's their sense of fairness because people attack them. As I've said, they're the only fish

I know about that will deliberately try to bite. Maybe there are others. Mainly though fish are only trying to escape."

"In the constant struggle between hunter and prey, I thought I was supposed to be the hunter," explained Rin.

"That theory is reliable except when you catch a shark," countered Cory.

"Would you like to dine on shark?" Rin asked.

"Thanks for the offer," he replied. "However, I've just started fishing and would like to see what other selection is on the menu."

"I like shark," offered a bystander who had approached unnoticed during the action.

Turning to see the woman, Rin said, "Well then, you have a fine shark for a number of meals and I guarantee this fish is fresh."

"If it was any fresher, I'd get bitten," joked the woman before she received both parts of the fish. "I never know what I'll discover when I go for a walk on the beach. Thank you. Dinner is heavy. I think I'll go home quickly."

Turning to Cory, Rin said, "Thanks for saving my thumb."

"You're gaining knowledge," said Cory before turning and starting to walk toward his equipment. Looking back, he added, "If you survive, you'll be wise."

"I didn't know knowledge about fishing was so difficult to obtain," replied Rin.

"All part of the fun," concluded Cory before walking again toward his equipment.

Rin collected his tackle then carried it back to his room. When everything had been looked after, he poured disinfectant over his wound before wrapping it with a bandage. Lastly, he carried two cans of beer to a chair beside his front door. He sat down, snapped open the first can, sipped the refreshing drink, and relaxed.

A gentle breeze rustled palm leaves and sent waves breaking along the sand. The sun started to set in a sky filling with deepening tints of pink, red and purple. Night was approaching, closing another segment of sunlight and opportunities. As beautiful as this world is, and although I keep knocking at its door to get in, I remain a stranger, an outsider, reflected Rin. I've been learning but only bits and pieces of something so much larger. With tomorrow's sunrise, I'll greet the new day at the breakfast and lunch restaurant. Afterward, I'll step forward on this great journey, hoping to advance beyond glimpses and start to see the real Gulf.

CHAPTER FOUR

COMPANION SEA

*R*in snapped open a second can of beer then sipped it contentedly while the setting sun withdrew beyond the horizon drawing away all deepening colors. Among night's shadows and rested by sounds of waves splashing upon the sand, Rin gradually left his thoughts and drifted into a deep sleep. He awoke briefly to find himself in light from the moon. It filled the sky and sent a path of silver to the beach.

The first rays of morning sunlight found Rin entering the breakfast and lunch restaurant. He sat at his usual table and was pleased to be greeted again by Jack.

"Good to see you at the start of a day," she said. "Menu?"

"A cheerful person like you helps start a day," he replied. "Just the same pancakes, grits, and coffee please."

"Right away," she declared before leaving and returning quickly with coffee. "How will you greet the day today?"

"I'm going to go for a particularly long walk along the shore to see if the rising sun and crashing waves will reveal some of their secrets in a way that will help me to feel less like a stranger to the sea. I've gone fishing but so far I feel like an outsider."

"I wish more people would seek their home with the environment so they would stop trying to destroy it," she explained. "Only a stranger, someone who does not understand the environment, would pollute it."

"It always helps to talk to a person, like you, who understands what I'm saying," he confessed.

"What started you on your fishing trip?" she enquired.

"A girlfriend, Amber Carlson," he answered. "She is a fishing guide who also fishes with other guides. She is part of the water and dumped me because I wasn't. She told me to go fishing—I might learn something. I've been trying but still feel like a stranger."

"We have to search to find and you are doing all you have to do—you are seeking," she observed. "I'd better go and search for your pancakes. They should be ready."

She walked away and returned with the food. "I hope your journey brings you the joy I've discovered," she added before walking away to greet other customers.

Rin felt renewed optimism when he left the restaurant. He parked his car at the resort then walked to the beach. Waves were rising up and cresting before crashing along the sand. Sandpipers, as usual, feeding on coquinas, searched backwashing flows. In one particularly high wave, sunlight outlined a passing school of fish. Rin recognized them as being mullet.

Getting into the harmony of waves splashing onto sand, Rin commenced his fast pace. He walked steadily, letting the music of water wash away worries.

This feels like a special day, he reflected as he moved past estates located back from the shore. He passed the crab shack. Gradually the estates also were left behind. He entered a shoreline that to him was new.

After he had gone beyond all buildings and entered what seemed to be an uninhabited area, he was surprised to see a person sitting on a bleached log at the water's edge. The person was fishing. His line stretched out to deeper, bluish-colored water. Beside him, there was a portable table. He was sipping a drink from one of two large cups. The other cup remained on the table. He was an old man with white hair and a beard. His eyes were bluish-green like the water. He said, "Welcome. It is time you got here. Some people take longer than others. You have for a long time been approaching. I invite you to sit down on this log and have a cup of coffee."

"You are a pleasant person to meet on the beach," said Rin before he sat down and reached for the cup. "Thank you."

"I thought you might like to sip a fine drink while I tell you a story," continued the man.

"Who wouldn't like to hear a story?" asked Rin. He sipped the drink and was amazed by its flavor, as it was more intriguingly pleasant than anything he had tasted previously. "Are you sure this is coffee?"

"Pure," answered the man. "That's the difference."

After pausing and looking out to the horizon, he continued, "I can tell you are searching. Most people are—although not all. That's why you came here—to earth—to learn what could not be experienced where there was no trouble and hardship. You picked this journey—not your girlfriend."

Rin felt pleasantly shocked because the words he heard awakened his spirit.

"You are here to develop and progress your spirit," continued the man. "All of life is spiritual and lives with the Creator. All creatures have a spark of the Creator. That's why people and creatures can understand each other. A person and a dog appear to be different but they are linked by a common spirit—and can become trusted friends. A similar link exists with all wild creatures. They can also understand us. If a person enters a forest and carries a gun for the purpose of killing, such a person will have difficulty finding wildlife. Enter the same woods with a camera or just for the pleasure of being there and life is yours to see. Why tell you all this? Well, you have asked. You wish to no longer be a stranger. Know then that the water, sea, and creatures are connected to you—are part of you. Realize that you belong and are not a stranger unless you choose to be. Walk to—seek the Creator and you see life. Walk away and you make your own hell. You seek the spirit. By being a seeker you have proven you are part of the Creator's life and not a stranger. You are thereby part of the sea, the fish, and other creatures."

"What is the right way to the Creator?" enquired Rin. "All groups, even different Christian groups, say they have the right—and only— way."

"Seek and you will find," answered the man.

"If wild creatures are connected to us, is it wrong for people to hunt them?" asked Rin.

"When the Europeans first came to this land, there was much wildlife and few hunters who actually needed food," replied the man. "So using wildlife—respectfully—for food was the natural way. Today there is little wildlife and many hunters so the time to hunt for food or furs is over. Wild creatures are few in numbers and have their own lives to live. Animals and birds used now for food and furs—and hunting—must be raised for this purpose."

"You are fishing," noted Rin. "Is it now wrong to go fishing?"

"Fish are more like plants," explained the man. "If they are in sufficient numbers, they can be harvested as long as such gathering is done respectfully and if not too many are taken. Fish and plants are also raised for food."

"So I am not a stranger?" asked Rin.

"You proved that by seeking not to be," answered the man. Rin felt a tingling sensation course through him, leaving him feeling awakened to life. I know, he thought, I'll never be the same again. I have been healed from my own lack of seeing.

With a new view of life exploding all around him, Rin really saw things for the first time and he knew his awareness was true. A shiver coursed through him again when he looked back, the old man along with everything he had with him, was gone.

Partly in a daze, Rin continued walking along the beach, feeling its companionship and seeing what was around him in a different way, in a new light. Wow, what a day, he thought. How could I ever explain this to someone else? I could say I feel at home now in the wilderness and am no longer a stranger.

He started walking back toward the resort. I have changed, he concluded. I now see my environmental surroundings with new respect and also enjoy the company.

Waves crashed to shore as they had always done and Rin walked with them, letting the song of the water envelope him. He proceeded onward, moving with the waves.

He entered the crab shack and Reg, with his reddish complexion brightening and an extra glint in his eyes, asked, "Dumped again?"

"No," Rin answered calmly before he sat at the bar. "I've been accepted. It's all a matter of how we see things and I now see life differently."

"What happened to the old Rin?" continued the bartender. "Did you leave him out there?"

"He's still here," he said. "He has just advanced—having more awareness of the way things are yet, previously, I just couldn't see them."

"Maybe someday you could explain all this to me," suggested Reg after he had poured a glass of draft and served it.

"I will always try," he said before sipping the drink. "Maybe we could add one of your healthy burgers."

"Coming right up," Reg exclaimed before walking to the window and placing the order. He put another glass of draft in front of Rin then had to take care of other customers.

The second draft was enjoyed more slowly along with the burger when it arrived. After he paid the bill and left a good tip, he resumed walking back to the resort.

He assembled his fishing equipment then walked to the water's edge. Having placed the chair and bait bucket, he gathered the cast net and was pleased when the first toss came back shinning with minnows.

Those are scaled sardines, he noted. Many people call them green backs. They're good bait. When he put them in the bucket some squirmed onto the sand and Rin noticed he had acquired two fishing friends—a snowy egret and a great blue heron. They helped tidy up loose minnows and also enjoyed others from the bucket. Rin named the heron, Iggy, and the egret, Henrietta. Henrietta chased away other egrets yet accepted Iggy. The heron also accepted the egret although could not be approached by other great blue herons.

Using a green back for bait, Rin started his first fishing trip. When minnows splashed at the surface farther out from shore, he tossed his bait into the splashes. Immediately something struck. The fishing pole throbbed as Rin brought to shore a slim, silvery-colored ladyfish. This first catch went to the heron. The fish, head first, went down the bird's long neck. More minnows were given to the egret.

The fishing pole again sent bait out to deeper, bluish-colored water. Waiting started. The three fishermen watched the water while its life continued in usual patterns. Pelicans soared above waves and occasionally dove for fish. Gulls struggled for a share of food. Porpoises moved past breaking through the surface at regular intervals. Another ladyfish went to the heron while the egret received extra minnows.

Life of the sea continued and the sun crossed the sky before Rin's pole sprang into action. Gradually he brought to shore a fine fish, a flounder.

He was unhooking the catch when Cory arrived. This time he carried a metal detector rather than fishing equipment. "You're fishing differently today," said Rin, in greeting.

"Yes," Cory replied. "There's as much to catch on land as in the sea. Sand and water both hold secrets, often parts of the same story. History is in both places and stories are unending."

Rin dropped the flounder into the bucket then asked, "What has been your best catch on land?"

"Pottery and arrowheads," Cory answered. "We're sort o' on the border between the Timucuas who used to live more northward in Florida and the Calusas who lived more southward. Both were numerous and were here when the Spaniards started arriving. Spaniards treated the Indians with brutality throughout the Americas and ransacked great civilizations, burning cities containing libraries and hospitals. Much has been lost. Gold especially was stolen and melted into coins that were taken back to Spain. Treasure ships were often destroyed by storms. There are gold coins, among other parts of history, in this sand. The worst scourges Spaniards brought to the Americas were new diseases and they greatly reduced Indian populations. I have found the misnamed Spanish gold coins—actually Indian or Indigenous gold—along with present day valuables—like cash and rings."

"You do as well fishing with a metal detector as with a pole," observed Rin.

"There are catches to be had in water and sand," added Cory. "I see you have done well today."

"Yes," agreed Rin. "Actually this day has gone beyond my wildest hopes and dreams."

"You're a fisherman now," declared Cory before he started to walk along the beach.

"As you are," added Rin. "I'm in great company—and I have a fish to cook."

Using remnant minnows, Rin completed feeding the heron and egret. Contented, they flew from the beach to resume their lives as they were lived in other locations.

Rin assembled his equipment then walked to his room where he filleted the flounder. Afterward, he drove to a store to get cooking supplies. Upon his return, he shook the fillets in a bag containing cornmeal before dropping the coated meat into a pan slightly covered with low-fat oil. In another pan, he fried some previously boiled and sliced potatoes.

Having sprinkled malt vinegar on the cooked fillets, he added them to a plate containing fried, sliced potatoes. Lastly, he added a dash of salt along with pepper before he sat down to enjoy the best food prepared so far at the resort.

Following the meal, he sat outside and sipped beer while he enjoyed considering his surroundings in new ways. He noticed that the heron was watching him from the resort's roof while the egret also adorned an adjacent railing.

Being part of the environment, as I am now, reflected Rin, along with respecting and helping it, enriches all life including myself. I must help other people to join and also enjoy my new way of seeing and experiencing the natural world.

Rin continued to sip a beer while evening colors changed to night's shadows. Again, he slept in his comfortable chair.

The first light of dawn found Rin and his two fishing partners at the water's edge where line stretched out into deep water. For variety, the first bait used was a previously frozen shrimp. The greenbacks netted had been shared between the bait bucket and the egret while the heron had enjoyed mullet that had also been caught in the net. Additional minnows and mullet were saved separately. They would be frozen for some of the next days when Iggy and Henrietta would want meals.

A strong hit on the bait sent the pole into action and following a good struggle, Rin brought to shore a large, perch-like sheepshead. After feeding the birds again, Rin carried his equipment along with his catch of the morning to the resort. He had a fine fish to fillet and other mullet and minnows to freeze for the birds.

With all projects completed, he prepared another delicious meal of cornmeal coated fillets fried until they were a dark golden color. Sliced potatoes were also fried to become part of an extraordinary meal savored outside while Rin sat on his favorite chair.

After washing dishes, Rin assembled his paint supplies in order to try painting again. He left his room and soon was setting up a chair and easel on the beach. Next to them, he placed paints and other equipment. Lastly, he sat down to select a brush.

First, he colored a board with basic hues of blue for sky and water along with tan for sand. Afterward, the actual picture was started whereby Rin picked colors from his surroundings and added them to the board, blending the shades in exact replicas of encircling life. The resulting scene depicted not just a scene of objects but also a portrayal of life.

Two women tourists were walking past just as the painting was finished. They saw in the depicted scene a representation of the spirit of wildness that had brought all the joy and excitement to their holiday. They wanted to buy this spirit and bring it back home with them so their holiday could be enjoyed not just once but every time the picture was seen. They bought the picture and afterward Rin's paintings kept being purchased as quickly as they could be painted.

During the following days, Rin followed what had started to be a routine with the first rays of morning sunlight finding him sitting on a chair at the water's edge. Having a bait bucket on one side and equipment on the other, he held a fishing pole while he watched the water as his line slanted down into greenish-blue depths. As always too, Iggy and Henrietta were constant companions.

One morning, after watching the heron beside him leave while another heron resumed the vigil, Rin realized that Iggy was actually a pair of herons although the two did not appear together—except to change shifts. One must always have to be at a nest, Rin concluded. Maybe Henrietta is also a pair of snowy egrets. They are of course also herons.

According to the morning ritual, the birds fed first. Henrietta had minnows while Iggy enjoyed small fish, particularly mullet, ladyfish, and sometimes whiting. People like whiting for food noted Rin. They are however a smaller fish and usually just the right size for Iggy.

A hit on the line started the pole dancing while the three fishermen braced for action. Rin was disappointed to see his line bringing to shore another catfish. People also use catfish for food, he thought as he carefully avoided the barbs while removing the hook. I don't favor these sail cats only because the serrated barbs are so dangerous.

Soon after the first catch, the pole bent with another strike. The following battle was long and slow again leading to disappointment. This time the catch was a stingray. Rin pulled it to shore then used a chair's leg to flip the creature over onto its back. After the hook was removed, the ray was turned over again before getting pushed into the water.

I'm going to change my hook and sinker arrangement concluded Rin, because I'm catching too many bottom-feeding fish. Some of them are good but I'm getting too many stingrays and sail cats. Rather than leave the hook at the end of the line with the sinker up higher so the bait rests on the bottom, I'm going to put a sand sinker at the end of the line. This sinker's triangular shape enables it to grip the sand. I'll place the hook farther up the line to be made more visible for fish swimming past and less noticeable to bottom feeders.

"Well Iggy and Henrietta," said Rin to his two companions, "we are now ready to do some serious fishing."

The line was again sent out into bluish depths. In a short time, the pole bent and jumped wildly as a fish fought all the way to shore. Seeing a sleekly shaped, beautifully colored, silvery form, Rin exclaimed to his friends, "A Spanish mackerel."

After unhooking the mackerel and placing it in the bait bucket, Rin gave the birds some minnows and mullet. These fishermen flew away just as Cory Woods approached.

"I suggest you should try fishing on land in addition to the water," he announced. "The sand holds as many stories and treasures as the sea. A fishing pole catches the present. A metal detector catches the past."

Giving Rin one of two detectors he carried, Cory continued, "You can keep this. It's of very good quality. I just don't use it anymore. It buzzes when metal has been located along with showing you what type it is and how far down it is buried. I hope the detector brings you as much enjoyment and treasure as I have discovered. Recently, I've only been using this other detector."

"Very considerate and generous of you," exclaimed Rin, accepting the gift.

"I'm on my way now to do some fishing on land," noted Cory before starting to walk farther along the beach.

"Hope you catch something," countered Rin. "I'm going to take my catch up to the room and do some filleting."

The two fishermen walked in different directions. Rin entered his room and filleted the mackerel. After putting the meat in the refrigerator, he drove to the breakfast restaurant.

He entered the building and sat in his usual chair where the table provided a view of the entire restaurant. Jack brought him coffee and announced, "Pancakes and grits have been ordered." Her blondish hair and greenish eyes seemed to match the spirit of optimism brightening her young face.

"You're like the morning itself," replied Rin. "You seem to be always bright with optimism—like the dawn of a new day."

"Each day is an opportunity," she added. "You seem to be especially optimistic yourself as if you started not just a new day but the dawn of your true road in life."

"You're insightful," he observed. "I have started a new dawn. I've entered your world of the environment with all its creatures."

"I can see there's something different about you," she confirmed.

"I'm not a trained scientist as you will be although I can support the environment by helping people to appreciate it, value it—and wake them up so they will stop destroying the natural world."

"Instead of just going fishing, now you'd be a good fishing guide," she observed before leaving to get the pancakes.

When they were placed on Rin's table, he said, "Thank you for your insight about the fishing guide idea."

"Likely that's the next step," she confirmed. "Welcome to our group."

"I appreciate the good company," he added, smiling with confidence since he felt sure a great new piece of his life had just dropped into place.

Rin enjoyed the meal—a fine start to a new day—and a new way of life. He paid the bill, adding the usual, large tip. Leaving the building, he walked into warming sunlight.

Back at the resort, Rin approached his room while Iggy and Henrietta waited by standing on outside chairs. When he entered the room, he noticed movement outside the window. He looked out the door and saw the heron peering around a corner of the building to see if this human fisherman was going to go out the back.

Inside his room, collecting fishing equipment, Rin happened to look out the door's window and saw the heron peering down from the roof to see where the fisherman had gone.

Rin carried his equipment to the beach where he was met by the heron and egret. He fed them first with minnows, in addition to some mullet, before settling down to watch line slanting into bluish depths while small waves danced across the surface.

When the pole bent and throbbed wildly, Rin waited while line was released then wound it back during a struggle that eventually brought to shore a sleek, king mackerel. After the next cast brought in another mackerel, Rin had enough fish for the day. He saved remaining minnows and mullet to give to the birds later—usually in the dark before the dawn.

Returning to his room, he put away equipment, filleted the two fish, and dusted some pieces with cornmeal after saving others for future use. A meal was prepared consisting of fried potatoes along with golden-colored fillets sprinkled with malt vinegar.

Following the meal, Rin decided to try using the metal detector. He carried it to the beach and started walking northward. A few clouds drifted across a pale blue sky where the usual patrols of pelicans moved above the restless Gulf. A flock of ibises flashed brightly across a wide panorama of blue. Small waves broke along the beach.

Some days—maybe every day if we could see them—the world seems perfect, reflected Rin as he strode forward into an increasing breeze. This same movement of air provided sufficient maneuverability for a sight he would never forget. Beside him, with wings outstretched in full majesty, the heron was gliding. The slight oncoming breeze made little wing movement necessary as Iggy glided next to Rin while they both proceeded along the beach.

Fully grasping the unbelievable moment, Rin continued walking and heard other people on the beach gasp at the sight. Someone said, "Look at the guy and the heron."

After a while, not wanting to get Iggy into another heron's territory where a fight would occur, Rin turned to go back. He started walking while Iggy flew ahead. They met at the resort.

When Rin sat down on his outside chair to sip beer while he watched the beach, he thought, the natural world is so much more incredible than many people realize. Amazing how smart creatures are. They are so much more than just a programmed series of actions. I can't identify Iggy or Henrietta when they are with other herons. However, when I'm on a beach, crowded with other people, both of these birds can identify me and will fly over to stand beside me.

Afternoon colors brightened to become the sunset before gradually becoming lost amid night's shadows. Rin slept soundly in his chair. He awoke to greet the dawn and welcomed a new day.

Returning to the restaurant for breakfast, he sat in his usual chair by the table providing a view of the beach where the morning sun was spreading golden light across sand and water.

"Good morning," said Jack who had approached unnoticed.

"It certainly is," he replied before she placed coffee on the table.

"The sand and water had your attention," she observed.

"Yes," he agreed. "I've learned much on this journey. Maybe we now see our surroundings the same way. I have joined the club."

"You have," she confirmed with green eyes brightening. "People spend their lives trying to make money. The best way to be successful, including financial prosperity, is to leave the environment in its naturally beautiful state then people will pay to see such beauty. Rather than destroy nature, its power can be harnessed from solar, thermal, and wind energy."

"Along my journey," reflected Rin, "I've met life. Although we have a common, spiritual link with others, each individual is unique and, with this difference, experiences life in an original way—making particular choices. I'm not the same person I was when I started this trip. Now, for the first time, I see the spiritual side of wilderness and know I, like you, are part of it."

"You really have come a long way on your journey—much farther than just in miles," noted Jack. "The bell rang. Your pancakes are ready."

She walked quickly to the kitchen window and returned to place steaming food on the table in front of Rin. "Thank you," he said. "I forgot about the pancakes."

After enjoying the meal, he paid his bill, in addition to including the same large tip. Leaving the restaurant, he was welcomed by warming sunlight during the walk to his car.

At the resort, he assembled fishing tackle and carried it to the beach, arriving just in time to see an approaching cloud of screaming gulls mixed with terns and pelicans. Birds were diving for minnows splashing at the surface, likely driven there by feeding fish.

This cloud of life moved in front of Rin. When an opening appeared, he threw out the net then pulled to shore a bundle of greenbacks along with an amberjack. He put minnows in the bait bucket, gave some to Iggy and Henrietta then returned the others—and amberjack—to the water.

The screaming cloud of birds and frenzy of fish kept moving along the shore. While Rin baited his line, he watched Iggy stalk something where foliage and grass bordered the beach. The heron stopped, becoming like a statue before his long neck flashed downwards only to swing up again with beak grasping a squirming, black snake. After getting shaken, the black form went slack then gradually vanished head first down the heron's raised throat and neck.

Herons do well fishing on their own, thought Rin. They, like everyone, enjoy some help too.

The baited line again was sent through the air to deep water where the sinker dropped to the bottom, leaving the baited hook ready for a catch of the day.

With the line set, the day fell into a routine of waiting for the three fishermen. The birds had been well fed. Henrietta was full yet continued the fishing custom. Iggy was comfortable and must be waiting due more to interest than food. The sky was clear and storm-free as had been the case for many days. Pelicans drifted above small waves sent to shore by a slight, salty breeze.

The pole did not move but the line did. It started to drift sideways following the shoreline. Rin released line to allow it to move steadily away. Having waited sufficiently, he stopped sending out line and pulled sharply back on the pole to set the hook. A battle began with the pole bending to a full half-circle. A pattern started whereby line was pulled out before gradually being reeled back. Eventually, a fighting fish was maneuvered to shore where Rin saw he had caught a huge red drum or redfish.

Hoping to get something smaller for Iggy, Rin baited the line again and threw it toward some minnows splashing at the surface. Immediately, the pole throbbed with action while a slender ladyfish was pulled to shore. This was unhooked and tossed to Iggy who started sending the fish down the long neck.

Rin carried the redfish to the room where fillets were saved. He gave most of them to Flo, who as usual was sitting in a chair outside her office.

"Always knew you'd be a real fisherman someday," she announced while receiving the packaged fillets. "Thank you for your generosity. Are you using the scales?"

"No," he answered, surprised by her interest in scales.

"If you're not needing them, I'd like them," she said. "I make shell pictures. Drum scales are wonderful as they can be fashioned into flowers on my pictures."

"I'll be right back," he noted before returning to his room. He unwrapped a package and saved the scales.

He gave them to Flo who declared, "Most appreciated! Again, I always knew you were a fisherman."

"I enjoy your confidence," he replied. "I didn't know until recently."

"Haven't had scales for a long time," she observed. "Now I'll make some more pictures. I have lots o' shells—and the fillets are also appreciated." Looking upward, she added, "Some of your other happy customers are in their usual places, standing on the roof above your room."

"I like the company of all my customers," he noted before returning to his room. He picked up the metal detector and walked to the beach.

First, he lowered the sensitivity in order to not have the detector buzzing about little items such as bottle caps. He started to walk on the sand, stepping along a firm border kept wet by the action of waves. They were larger now, each one rising, cresting then crashing onto the shore. Water flowed in clear sheets before washing back to be replaced by the next crest. As had happened previously, sunlight shining through a rising wall of water outlined forms of fish swimming past. Sunrays also added a golden sheen to water and sky in addition to bringing warmth, balanced by a refreshing, salty breeze. It had increased to be a light wind as it crested larger waves and rustled leaves of palms back from the beach. Pelicans patrolled like necessary parts of a healthy sea. Gulls added their cries and white flashes to a pale blue sky.

These natural surroundings are all living, moving, and acting in harmony, aspects of one life, reflected Rin while he realized he traveled, not as an outsider, but as part of the wilderness that was the sea and its shore. There is one spirit in us all.

Caught and lifted by the harmony he had joined, he kept moving. I enjoy being absorbed in life I can now better understand, he concluded. Excitement remains because we can never comprehend completely. I have become part of the wind, water, sky, and sand, as we are all part of one spiritual life.

Listening to the song of his surroundings, he proceeded onward in a euphoric state of enjoyment until he was jolted by a loud buzzing sound. Stopping, he looked at his metal detector. He moved it around until it sounded particularly loudly at one place in the sand.

Rin ran his hand along the surface where waves reached their highest point. He started to dig, allowing the removed layer to be washed away by a receding wave. After the water had retreated, there remained a raised, circular object. Picking up the item, he thought, could be lead. If the detector is right, this is a gold coin and must be valuable. Spaniards in the Americas stole gold and silver from the Indigenous people while sacking their cities. Gold objects were melted into coins. Many ships carrying gold to Spain were lost at sea usually because of storms or attacks by the English. A ship must've been wrecked off this coast and its cargo has become part of the sand. This might be one remnant coin or maybe there are others.

Rin moved the detector around the area although there were no further soundings. He sat down on an eroded bank to rest while he watched a sailboat move with wind far out in the bluish tinged water.

When he leaned the detector against the bank, the instrument buzzed to its full volume. He stood up, checked the area around his feet yet there was no further response. Inadvertently, he moved the detector along the face of the bank and the alarm sounded as loudly as before.

Checking the bank's side, he noted horizontal lines of a different color, marking old shorelines. Storms and, particularly hurricanes, through the years change shorelines, he reasoned. One of these dark borders would mark the shore when the Spanish ship was wrecked.

Additional efforts clearly revealed one line, and only one, that caused loud responses. Selecting a piece of sturdy driftwood to use as a pry bar, he worked until he had cleared a large area. When the bank could activate no further soundings, he ran the detector over the removed sand and there was a continuously loud response.

He worked in disbelief as if he was caught in a dream he could not wake up from and the coins he uncovered were too real to be imaginary. Too excited to notice fatigue, he kept busy until he had a mound of what must be gold coins. A final check of the area revealed no additional reaction from the metal detector.

He filled his pack with coins then stretched out on the sand to finally rest. I can't deny this good luck has happened, he told himself while looking up at the sky just as an eagle soared overhead. There are times of tragedy we have to face. Also, there are opportunities—some are small while others are great. This is a great time. Such a gift I've received today is only half mine. I would not have thought of using a metal detector if Cory had not given me his spare machine. We are partners and he will receive half of this discovery. I'll go back to the resort, divide this treasure then take half to Cory. The natural surroundings that I now know I'm part of are in harmony and I walked here in this song. Reminded by such music, I know there is no such thing as coincidence. I was told to go fishing because I might learn something. This part of my journey is concluding and the northern part is about to begin. This treasure must be for the next section of the road. I can now afford to buy a boat. I'll become a fishing guide.

Walking back to the resort, the gold seemed to get heavier along the way. There's a lot of weight on my back, thought Rin, but I certainly don't carry a burden.

Approaching his destination, he saw in the distance the welcome form of Cory who was fishing. In the room, the treasure was divided equally into two packs. Carrying one of the bundles, Rin walked to the beach and proceeded toward the fisherman.

"How's fishing?" asked Rin.

"Nothing yet," Cory answered.

"Your catch today is not approaching you in the water but on the land," observed Rin.

"I look every day for something special that the morning sun will shine upon although a catch of the day arriving from the land makes this day unique—a golden fish," explained Cory.

"You must be psychic," replied Rin. "Your catch today is a golden fish. I used your metal detector and found gold coins. I wouldn't have found them if you had not done half of the preparation by giving me the detector. Half of what it found is yours and in this bag."

Receiving the heavy pack, Cory opened it, brought out one piece, rubbed it, bit a corner then exclaimed, "Thank you, yet I can't believe it. This is the catch of the day and what a catch."

Reaching into his pocket, Cory withdrew a golden replica of a fish. Holding it up, he explained, "I carry this golden fish always. It's my good luck charm—a replica, or symbol, of the best of days. Each special time I consider is a golden fish—the catch of the day, a week, a year, and, sometimes, a lifetime. That's what this gold is. It's a golden fish— the catch of a lifetime—and thank you for sharing."

"Without your metal detector, this discovery would never have happened," observed Rin.

"These coins are going to enable me to build a new sailboat to replace the one I lost when I had no insurance and got hit by a storm off Maui," noted Cory.

"You built your previous boat?" asked Rin.

"Yes," he replied while he put the golden fish back into his pocket.

"And sailed to Hawaii?" enquired Rin again.

"Yes," answered Cory. "I can now build a new boat and sail again to Hawaii. Storms are few and far between. The rest o' the time the weather is perfect. Some rooms I've rented had no heater and no air conditioner. There were just vents to let in the perfect climate."

Winding in his line, Cory said, "No more fishing today. Must look after the catch of a lifetime. People who use metal detectors, like me, know how to clean coins. I'll show you how to clean this treasure. Much of it—most of it—should go into banks."

"Good idea," agreed Rin.

Standing, Cory said, "If you want some help, bring your gold and come with me. We'll clean it then get it usable. I've had experience turning treasure into a usable bank account.

Rin accompanied Cory to his house. The treasure was prepared and, soon after, much of it was deposited in banks.

Having secured finances, Rin returned to the resort. He took his fishing equipment to the shore only long enough to catch food for Iggy and Henrietta. After looking after his fishing companions, Rin drove to the restaurant where Sophie worked. He sat in his usual place providing a view of docks painted this time in reddish hues from the setting sun.

Sophie approached, saying, "It's about time—stranger. For dessert today—on the house—you're getting my other specialty. What will you have first to accompany a glass o' draft?"

"Good to see you too," he replied. "A grouper sandwich please—with cheese."

"How's fishing?" she enquired.

"Couldn't be better," he exclaimed. "How's your other specialty?"

"There's nothing like it," she declared before leaving to place his order. She returned to put a glass of draft on his table.

"Thank you," he said. "You pour the best draft also."

"Of course," she declared before leaving Rin to sip a refreshing drink and consider the enormity of what had befallen him since he had been told to go fishing. I went fishing, he reflected, and caught a new life. I entered a world that previously I did not know existed. My work now will be to share what I have been taught about companionship with the environment. I'll invest some of my new finances into buying a boat then use it to become a guide for fishing along with photography, painting, and all ways of appreciating life in harmony with nature. Now that I've been given gifts, I know that part of them is the next step—sharing them with others.

The glass emptied and Sophie brought another. "You seem to have caught a few dreams too," she observed, noting he had not stopped watching the docks while their colors deepened as the sun set.

"I caught a golden fish," he replied. "A catch larger than anything I could have thought possible before setting out for this trip. I'm going to buy a boat and some property."

"I've always believed," affirmed Sophie, "our mountains are higher than our valleys are low. Time now for you to catch a grouper."

She walked to the kitchen window and returned carrying a requested grouper sandwich. After Rin had savored his specialty Sophie arrived with hers.

"That's it," she declared—warm syrupy, pecan pie topped with vanilla ice cream." She walked away, leaving him to try a treat that looked delicious and tasted like a combination of the finest flavors of the south.

Paying his bill and leaving the usual tip, he said, "Your specialty gives people a sample of the finest flavor of southern food. Your specialties are not just foods but experiences of the best flavors the south has to offer."

"I thought a real fisherman like you would appreciate the experience— and as always," she declared, "I'm always right."

"Thanks for the experience," he added before leaving and walking to his car amid remnant red tints left by the sunset.

CHAPTER FIVE

JOURNEY NORTH

After leaving the resort, Rin stopped at a gift shop and bought a replica of a golden fish. He attached this good luck charm to a fine, gold chain then wore it around his neck. Afterward, he continued driving to the airport and returned the rented car.

He later looked down at the airport and far beyond it there gradually appeared a view of the Gulf catching first coloring from the rising moon. Looking out at the stars and moon, Rin drifted into sleep and was awakened by the slight bump of the plane returning to a runway.

As had happened previously, he got a ride with the airport service to the apartment where he had lived. Nothing remained but his car. His apartment had been leased to others because all ties to him had expired. His few possessions were in boxes in an attendant's office.

After packing the boxes in his car, he started driving. I have completed a long journey in the south, he thought and looks like a new adventure has come into view with the trail pointing north.

This is a rare time in life, he reflected after sipping coffee purchased at a restaurant before turning onto the main highway. Almost instantly, the stimulating drink stirred his thoughts into the realm of dreams. I have an unusual opportunity now because there is apparently the freedom to turn in any direction and I have picked the northern route. Likely though there was no choice at all because I know I would not have selected any other destination. The main plan is more determined than we are aware and our choices mainly involve staying the course or turning away. I have made my decision and will stay on course.

As miles are traveled, he observed, the land becomes wilder. I have gradually entered a region of wilderness. In the south, I ventured into the wilderness of the sea where it touched the shore. In the north, the land is wild in addition to the water. I'll return to a place I visited in the past and remember having a feeling this area would play an important part in my life. Some earlier inhabitants, the Hurons, called the main water in the region, Lake of the Alligouautan. Champlain called it Fresh Water Sea. The Ojibway considered it, Spirit Lake. Generally today, this bluish-green, clean water is known as Georgian Bay.

The first view of the freshwater sea occurred at Parry Sound where Rin stopped at a restaurant providing a view of the harbor. He had ordered a glass of draft just before a boat stopped at the dock. This scene fit ideally with his plans and dreams.

That's exactly my kind o' boat, he noted. The sides are high. The deck looks like it, along with the rest of the vessel, could handle rough weather. Everything has been built to be practical—rather than fancy or beautiful.

The owner looks as seaworthy as his craft, thought Rin. He stood up, told the server he'd be back then rushed to the dock.

"Ever think of selling your boat?" Rin asked the weathered fellow who had just tied up his vessel.

"Only when I feel as old as I look," replied the guy with a glint in his gray eyes. They were set in a lined face that appeared to have looked often into sunlight dancing on waves. All his features, like his boat, seemed designed to be practical rather than attractive in any other way. Long gray hair was tied at the back of his head.

"I'm Rin—Rinton Fox, he said.

"Ben Canby," replied the guy before they shook hands.

"I was having beer and dinner upstairs," continued Rin. "I could buy the same for you and we could talk over some business."

"Ya talked me right into it," Ben replied with his lined face breaking into a smile.

Upstairs, they sat at the table where Ben received beer before they both checked menus. Rin said, "I was thinking of buying a boat like yours and becoming a guide to take people out for fishing, painting, or filming."

"That's what I've been doing," offered Ben.

"Do you think we could make a deal for selling your vessel?" asked Rin.

"I could spend more time looking after my outdoors store," Ben replied, obviously thinking things over. "The right amount for the boat would be the deal maker or breaker."

"I could pay in gold or cash," explained Rin.

"Gold?" he asked, showing a real interest for the first time. "I've been a prospector all my life. Didn't think I'd make my first strike in a restaurant."

"I made my strike with a metal detector and found some of these," Rin explained, reaching into his pocket. He withdrew a gold coin and extended it to Ben.

Receiving the coin, Ben observed, "That's got as much value in its history as in gold. The right number of those would get you my boat and everything that goes with it. I've been trying to make a gold strike all my life. I'm a hunter of gold—not fish."

"We can talk about numbers," said Rin, "and we'll get to the right one."

When the server returned both men ordered the whitefish special along with another draft. "I'm one of the volunteer rescuers," noted Ben. "That's something they'll probably ask you to do once you get established. You could continue where I leave off. You could take over my client list."

"I would be purchasing not only a boat but an established business?" enquired Rin.

"Yes," agreed Ben. Looking out past the docks to the Bay, he continued, "I think the most beautiful country and best fishing occurs where there are fewer people and that location is north of here. As you go north cottages are less numerous and there is more wilderness along with the most fish. I used to trawl for salmon but they seem to have gone. That's why you caught me at the right time. The salmon quit, and so I figured to do the same. Then you appeared showing me how to make the change. As I've said, I've always been a prospector and you're offering what I haven't been able to find. Never thought of lookin' in a restaurant. As they always say, "Gold is where you find it.""

"I keep discovering there's no such thing as coincidence," observed Rin.

"You talked me right into it," declared Ben before they raised their glasses to a new turn in a journey.

Walking back to his car, Rin concluded, I now own a boat I can use to guide. I'll continue to pay the insurance. Ben is going to send his previous customers to me. I'll also carry on his work with volunteer rescue. I'll take over costs for keeping the boat here at the marina. On the top floor, temporarily, I've rented a room. It provides a fine view of the harbor. I now have to move into my new residence. Afterward, I'll buy supplies and start getting to know this area so I can be a guide.

The room was old—as it was part of the region's history. Through many windows, there could be seen a panorama of the harbor with all accompanying sounds and scents.

After packing his boat with supplies, Rin bought maps and charts. Finally, he drove his new craft out of the harbor and into the main channel. I'll visit the islands first, he determined. Afterward, I'll explore the coast as it extends northward. I'll want to locate the best fishing places in addition to favorite areas for painting, filming, and even historic touring. I already know the history.

A journey among islands brought the bow of Rin's boat splashing across pristine water of the clearest tints varying from crystal clear when shallow to golden in the sunlight, light green with moderate depth, or more blue as depth increases. Islands were of every size and shape although were almost always of glaciated, smooth granite containing many colors at close range while blending into gray with distance.

I prefer uninhabited islands, noted Rin. I can bring people to them without concern for owners. The island I'm on now is particularly picturesque. Smooth rock leads to deep water where fishing must be good while painting would be spectacular.

After roping his boat to a dock, Rin thought, to use this site I'll need permission from the owner who has a plane located at a connecting island. Looks like the owner is approaching now, noted Rin when he saw a person leave a house on top of the island. As he loomed closer, Rin saw a man who was bald on top of his head while sides seemed shaved. He had blue eyes, a well-manicured gray beard, and a gold front tooth.

He was a formidable-looking character as all of his stature portrayed largeness, particularly his stomach.

"You the island's owner?" asked Rin of the man who now stood on the dock.

"That's right," stated the fellow crisply. "Who might you be?"

"Rin Fox," he answered. "As you can see, I've purchased Ben Canby's boat—and business. He said you approved of people being brought here for fishing, painting, or filming. You are Charles Stewart?"

"Yes," he replied. "If you're as good as Ben at taking care of the place, you can continue to bring people here. I own a beautiful part of Georgian Bay and if visitors are respectful of the island I'll share it with people I know. Ben approved of you or he would not sell you his business and tell you about me. His judgment means you're welcome."

"I didn't know his approval of me was part of the deal," observed Rin.

"That's the only part of the deal," stated Charles. "People have been trying to buy Ben's business for as long as I've known him."

"I might add that he also recommended you," said Rin. "Ben didn't stop at other privately owned islands and I won't either."

"There are a lot of uninhabited places," confirmed Charles.

"I'm out exploring them now," added Rin. "How can I repay or thank you for your generosity? Ben said he left fresh fish—catch o' the day—in your freezer. Each package was labeled with the type of fish and the date caught."

"That tradition can continue," affirmed Charles. "And if I like a painting done on this island I get to keep it?"

"That's a good tradition too," said Rin.

"I'll show you how to get into the building when I'm not here," offered Charles before he started walking back upward along gradually sloping rock. Rin followed while he admired the view opening up with each step leading higher. "Everything on this island is locked," continued the large man. "Only one thing will open."

He walked to a window, lifted it upward then stepped inside. Rin followed as they entered a vast room. There were card and roulette tables in a bar where windows filled much of each wall. A central feature was a stone fireplace.

"Occasionally people come in here if they are caught in a storm or need a washroom," explained Charles. "This is the entertainment area. I have another cottage where I park my plane."

"Good of you to share all this," said Rin.

"Sometimes I enjoy having visitors," noted Charles.

"This visitor has enjoyed meeting you," said Rin. "I should carry on with my tour to continue learning about Ben's business so I can resume guiding his customers."

"You're already most o' the way there," confirmed Charles.

"Thank you," replied Rin as he started to follow Charles back to the dock. After untying his boat, Rin stepped inside.

"What kind of paintings do you like?" asked Rin.

"Anything about this island," came the answer.

"Appreciate your hospitality," said Rin before starting the motor. He turned the bow toward a horizon dotted with islands.

He resumed exploring a region that, as had happened in the south, opened up and allowed him to enter, even welcomed him, revealing beauty at every turn including the best fishing places along with almost endless vistas that are beyond the reach of any camera's limit, or painter's brush. The beyond limits realm, reflected Rin, is what is most attractive to the best photographers, painters, or fishermen. Artists can be classified according to how far they can go in the accuracy of depiction in their work. Although the full depth of discovery is actually viewed by very few.

During certain glimpses beyond physical boundaries, Rin could see what he enjoyed most and that was the spiritual, sacred connection. Here he had companionship beyond the reach of a camera, paintbrush—or even fishing pole.

Again, just as I discovered in the south, observed Rin while he camped on one of the islands, I'm at home here. I have a responsibility to share with others—or at least attempt to reveal—the truest view of the natural world that people too often don't see in their pursuit of economic benefits. The water here is pure and money can't restore this aspect to a lake, or river, used as a dump for small economic gain. Only by working with nature can there be true prosperity.

CHAPTER SIX

THE GUIDE

*B*en Canby advised his customers to continue with the new guy, Rin Fox. The first to arrive were artists from Toronto. They came to camp, as had become their custom, on an uninhabited island. They brought their tents and equipment while Rin provided transportation to the island. He enjoyed watching the progress of their pictures. He was like a shadow drifting at the edge of this self-contained group. On the way back from their camp, they wanted to stop, as they usually did, at Stewart's Island where they swam in the crystal clear water and basked in the sun.

The artists were a happy group when they returned to the dock at Parry Sound. Rin's new career had started.

The next customers were two young men also from the city. Their parents, as previously, paid for their fishing trip. One, called Jody, had well-trimmed, black hair and eyes of the same color. There was a sleek quality to his overall appearance. The other guy, known as Roger, was the opposite in every way although he had the same color of hair and eyes. He was overweight and generally scruffy.

Rin always supplied fishing equipment and the two men supplied their case of beer.

After leaving the harbor, Rin set up each customer with a trawling line. In a short time, the day settled into a routine filled with an expectation, almost a promise, of action.

When his pole bent and thrashed, Jody joined in the battle just before a large bass broke from the surface and tossed the bait skyward. "That was fun," he exclaimed as Rin started resetting the line.

"Bass are like that," said Rin. "They really fight. When they jump, they usually throw the hook."

"Calls for a beer," noted Roger before he opened the case. "You have a washroom on this boat?" he asked Rin.

"Yes," he answered. "Lower deck."

"Good," said Jody while he received a beer from Roger. "With this beer, we're goin' to be needin' one. Want a beer?" he asked Rin.

"Not now," he answered. "Thanks."

Trawling settled into some of the tranquility and infinite peacefulness that a day of fishing usually brings until Rin saw an empty beer bottle leave his boat, rise up into the air along an arcing course ending with a splash in greenish-blue water.

"If that happens again, this fishing trip is over and won't start again until you know how to respect the environment," stated Rin with a steely tone to his voice. Anger flashed when he saw a second, empty bottle shoot skyward before splashing into the water.

"I don't repeat advice," Rin stated before he started reeling in the lines.

"You're paid to take us fishing," complained Jody, struggling to believe what was happening.

"Not enough," Rin countered after he stored the first pole then started working with the second.

"You were paid a lot of money to take us fishing," flared Roger.

"I was paid to take you fishing but not to take you polluting," stated Rin, feeling the full grip of anger. "If you want me to tell you about respecting the environment I will inform you. That's why I take people out here on these trips. Money just looks after expenses—doesn't cover purpose! This is one of the dwindling wilderness regions in the world. The water is clean. It isn't a place to throw trash."

"We have nothing to learn from you," stated Jody.

The return trip was silent except for a steady drone of the motor combined with the whispering splash of water as it curled away from the moving craft. At the dock, the two customers took their beer and left. After stopping at the restaurant, Rin walked to his rented room. Looking through the windows at the harbor, he sipped beer slowly and felt satisfied with his day's work.

The next day, darkening skies and increasing wind blocked the possibility of a customary trip. Signals of bad weather to come were fulfilled when a storm struck.

Storms in life come and go, thought Rin while he prepared his boat to leave the safety of the harbor. Some storms last a lifetime. Others pass. When the Coast Guard called and said all other boats were out on calls so would I try to rescue two people in a sinking sailboat northwest of Stewart's Island, I knew this storm would last a lifetime for me if I didn't try to help.

Workers watched in silence as Rin steered his boat out of the harbor. Afterward, he turned his craft to face the full fury of the storm.

Seeing what he was up against, Rin reasoned, I know I, and all people, should work with the environment and never against it. I seem to be going against it today but I'll try to work with it too and maybe we'll survive. I don't think I had a choice. I could not have refused to help.

The fury of this storm is something I have not experienced previously or even imagined. I've heard others talk about it.

He felt the tensing of raw fear as he looked into the watery darkness. There was little distinction between sky and waves. General inkiness brightened with lightning before each crash of thunder that was muted by waves pounding against the boat.

The craft would climb one precipice to its foaming summit only to drop into a trough. Rin felt a constant dread that the bow might not point upward in time to avoid being swallowed by the next wall of water. As long as there continues to be some pattern to waves, he reasoned, I'll slant the bow into them, rather than hit one directly. I'm amazed by how my mind works so clearly when it's forced to focus. Taking one second at a time with each wave handled well, I'll keep doing everything possible to find the stricken boat. Only foaming water adds some white to the murkiness of the sky and water. I don't see the environment as an enemy and this knowledge is likely my greatest strength in dealing with such a storm, he resolved while continuing to maneuver his craft. I have also acquired skills although they seem a little puny when faced with such a struggle.

Almost not believing the sight, Rin saw the sailboat when it was lifted up by a wave. He mustered all his ability to maneuver his craft beside the stricken vessel, allowing time for two people, wearing life jackets, to scramble aboard.

"Each of you put on one of those backpacks—like I'm wearing!" he shouted. "Each pack carries emergency supplies! Hang on to this boat!"

Feeling some relief and exhilaration after finding the people, Rin now turned his boat back and tried to ride with the waves, following each mountainous wall as it dropped into a foaming trough before another wall formed. He focused on each obstacle—nothing else mattered. I can only hope, he concluded, the waves continue to hold to a steady course. The boat is managing to ride the crests and come out of each valley.

Rin's feeling of elation after finding the people started to vanish when he saw the waves losing any pattern. Walls of water started appearing from all directions, making attempts to keep the bow above each crest impossible. The boat dropped into a seething opening. The bough was pointing downwards when it vanished under an advancing wall.

Rin struggled underwater. When he broke through the surface, he gasped for air then saw the other people struggle above the foam. He attached them to a line. Each one worked to breathe while life jackets supplied buoyancy.

The battle for breath continued timelessly until the three people were thrown onto smooth rocks. Backwashing water sent the stragglers back into waves twice before a particularly large wall of water washed them farther up onto the shore. Reacting immediately, they scrambled away from the water's grip.

Grateful to feel solid rock beneath them, they rested and gave in to exhaustion. Eventually, the two rescued people stirred. They walked toward Rin who was sitting on an outcropping of rock.

"You saved our lives," said the rescued man. "We will be forever grateful."

"We had more than me watching out for us in that storm," said Rin. "This was not our time to die."

"My wife is Catherine—Cathy," said the man. "I'm Casper—or Cas—Woodstock.

"And we couldn't be happier or more grateful to meet you," exclaimed the woman who had bright blue eyes. Graying brown hair was tied at the back of her head into a long braid. Her face was lined, showing both softness and strength. The man also had blue eyes, strong facial features, and gray hair. Both people were tall.

Shouting into a particularly strong gust of wind, Rin said, "We must stay in sight of each other. Always know where the others are. Don't wander away by yourself and get lost. We have to find a sheltered place, make camp and get dry."

Always being aware of the location of the other two, Rin started walking along a treeless expanse of smooth rocks. At the end of this area, he turned southward, entering a section of forest offering some protection from wind and rain.

At the base of a rock wall, he stopped. Eastward, a flat base of rock dropped down to a creek that would be flowing into Georgian Bay.

Turning to Cathy and Cas, Rin said, "This rock wall will protect us from the storm—and falling trees. "I'm going to build a lean-to shelter. You could sit down and check your backpacks. In them, you'll find a compass, all-purpose coffee pot, frying pan, cooking oil, coffee, and knife along with matches, rope, medical kit, and water-purifying pills. There's also basic food and fishing equipment. Check your compasses and always know the directions. We will be walking southward, following the shore."

"Do you know where we are?" asked Cas.

"We have to be on the coast, north of Parry Sound," he answered. "We'll walk southward until we meet someone."

"They'll be looking for us?" enquired Cathy, her face looking particularly pale from cold and shock.

"The Coast Guard asked me to rescue you," noted Rin. "They didn't say I also had to rescue your boat or mine," he added smiling.

"Oh—that explains it," exclaimed Cas in mock alarm. "I wondered why we left them behind."

"You guys are joking around in a situation like this?" gasped Cathy.

"Storms come in life," added Rin. "It's how we handle them that counts. Now we need a shelter. Please check the equipment in your packs. Waste nothing."

He removed a small hatchet from his pack and started trimming poles from a network of dead trees that had fallen or were easy to knock over. He leaned each pole against the rock wall, making a shelter, open at one end where there would be the main fire. A second, small fire would be located inside the lean-to next to the cliff.

After the poles were neatly in place, he covered them with balsam and hemlock boughs. He also prepared a floor of boughs before lastly building a small, inside fire in addition to a tall blaze outside in front of the shelter's open end.

With outer clothing drying on ropes beside fires, Cathy smiled for the first time and said, "I didn't think I'd ever be warm again. Thank you, Rin for always saving us."

"I'm as happy as you are that you are both well," said Rin. "We do what we have to do—and sometimes we're successful. Was your boat insured?"

"Yes," she stated. "Was Yours?"

"Yes," he replied.

"We're not insured," added Cas, smiling.

"If you're not insured, I suppose I should try to get you out of here safely," stated Rin.

"We are already forever grateful," exclaimed Cathy who seemed to have almost forgotten the storm.

"How did you two get stranded?" asked Rin.

"We took shelter behind an island," explained Cas. "It turned out to be too low for real protection because the wind swept right over it and took us off our anchorage. We were almost instantly in trouble and we called for help."

"Don't suppose you have a phone now?" asked Rin.

"They're somewhere in Georgian Bay," said Cathy with her eyes darkening.

"Where were you planning to sail?" enquired Rin again.

"Casper always wanted to sail all along the shore of the most beautiful lake in the world—Georgian Bay," answered Cathy.

"We haven't been sailing for long," observed Cas, "but long enough to try for the Bay."

"The trip was beautiful while it lasted," observed Cathy," with her eyes brightening again.

"Well, you both face adversity well," stated Rin. "Trouble will always come. It's how we react to it that counts."

"You're volunteer rescue?" asked Cas

"Yes," he replied.

"You volunteered to go out in a storm like this?" Cas enquired again.

"No," he answered. "Like the birds, animals, and even fish, I remain in camp during a storm. I was asked to go out and get you—so I had no choice."

"Your lack of choice saved our lives," stated Cas.

"That's why we're all happy despite our present situation," observed Rin. "Actually I'm at home here—storm or sunshine. The wilderness of lakes and forest is paradise, particularly when compared to a city."

"Good to hear you feel at home here," noted Cathy.

"Yes," he affirmed. "Your first meal will be tea and biscuits—served soon."

"Sounds like a banquet," exclaimed Cathy, smiling brightly.

Assembling two pots, Rin filled them with clear, cold water from the stream. In a short time, water was boiling. This process continued while Rin made other preparations. After sufficient boiling, tea was served accompanied by biscuits.

"This meal and accommodation are more appreciated than any we've had in the past," noted Cas.

"Warm again—and dry—with food and tea—along with the best cook in the world," continued Cathy.

"Pleased to hear you enjoy my cooking," observed Rin. "Maybe tomorrow night we'll be dining on fried fish."

"You can catch fish near this camp?" asked Cas.

"No," answered Rin. "But possibly at the next camp."

"Oh," sighed Cathy. "We'd better get some rest then—and sleep."

"You're going to need both," affirmed Rin.

Each traveler settled in for the night. The storm gradually diminished bringing darkness and silence.

Morning sunlight shone on the three people while they walked southward next to the coast. Traveling was easiest along rocky stretches of shoreline. Forested areas were more challenging. The greatest obstacles were the marshes. Pushing through water sometimes chest-deep brought back wet clothing that gradually became almost a normal condition.

The next camp was again established behind a high stretch of rocks topped by jack and white pines. This site was selected because Rin saw the possibility of catching fish. Rocks bordering a small bay dropped into deep water.

After preparing a lean-to shelter, he caught crayfish and used them for bait. His extension, fishing pole sent the baited line out from a rock outcropping into deep, greenish-blue water. The bait slowly sank then was retrieved and sent out again.

We have dried soups and beans, recalled Rin. Fresh fish is always a delicacy and would be especially appreciated now.

He felt a flush of excitement when something strong struck the bait. The line moved upward through the water before a large bass exploded from the surface. Flashing silver and green hues, the battler shook from side to side before returning to bluish depths leaving behind a slack line.

We could have used that food, thought Rin, hit by disappointment. When he started retrieving line, it resisted as the fish darted out from a rock shelter and again shot to the surface at the center of the arcing spray. Submerging again, the fish continued to fight.

Gradually Rin pulled the bass to an area of low rocks where he brought the catch up onto a patch of grass. "A prize fish at any time," he exclaimed.

He took the fish a long way from camp and prepared fillets. While he was working, a sleek, dark brown mink rambled along the shore until catching a crayfish then crunched loudly while devouring the snack. Afterward, the visitor approached and picked up some extra fish parts left on a rock for hungry travelers.

Back at camp, Rin fried the fillets. He sprinkled them with malt vinegar, in addition to salt and pepper, before serving them on birch bark plates. Afterward, he added tea.

Enjoying the meal, the three people sat within warmth provided by a tall fire outside the lean-to. Beyond the flames, the wilderness gathered to itself red hues from the setting sun. A calm came to the area where no movement was discerned other than lengthening shadows. Night arrived revealing a vast array of stars above the camp. Clear calls of a whippoorwill spoke repeatedly. Afterward, an owl called.

"That's the best fish I've had," exclaimed Cas.

"Oh Casper!" declared Cathy.

"Except for your cooking of course," he added, trying to cover his mistake.

"Don't worry," she replied. "Best fish I've ever had too,"

"Circumstances affect the taste," observed Rin. "We can burn the plates. Keep saving your knives and forks. I'll wash the pans."

When Rin returned from cleaning the pans, he served more tea. The three people were sitting around the fire, enjoying tea when wolves howled.

"Wilderness," said Casper. "I don't think I've ever been in it before—not on land. I've been there on the water. I've seen wilderness on land but never actually been there and the sensation is stirring interests I didn't even know I had."

"It has helped to have a great cook and fishing guide with us," observed Cathy.

"Yes," he agreed. "Have you always been a fishing guide?" he asked Rin.

"No," he answered. "I worked in an office. I had a girlfriend whom I thought was the right one. She broke things off and told me to go fishing because I might learn something. Well, I went fishing. I either became the person I really was all the time—and I think this was the case—or I changed—never to be the same again. Now I'm a fishing guide, doing volunteer rescue work and also painting."

"Cas and I both like to paint," noted Cathy.

"What was your girlfriend's name," Cas asked Rin.

"Amber Carlson," he replied.

"You haven't heard from her since she told you to go fishing?" Cas asked again.

"No," he answered. "Lost contact. Don't know where she is. I've had a hard life and seem to learn things that way."

"Life is harder for some people than others," noted Cas.

"What kind of work do you two do when you're not sailing?" asked Rin.

"Stockbroker," he replied. "Made a lot o' money in stocks."

"Lost a lot too," added Cathy. "But made more than lost. I was a librarian. We both paint. This trip is something Casper, particularly, always wanted to take."

"Has been a lot more exciting than expected," declared Cas. "This wilderness area is the most beautiful region in the world. People have not ruined it."

"Although other nomadic people were here before them, the best remembered are the Ojibway," explained Rin. "According to traditions, they came from the east and kept moving westward likely because the Iroquois were to the south. Ojibway live here today. Fur trading activity increased with Europeans' demand for furs, especially beaver, used to make felt hats. Loggers came, cutting down mainly white pine along with others too like hemlock. Farming has been attempted but the region has never been good for growing crops. The land is too rocky and the growing season is too short.

Maybe there was a need for trapping and hunting in the past when food supplies were sparse, wildlife was plentiful and there were only a small number of hunters. Today, the opposite has occurred. There are alternative sources for food, wildlife is scarce and hunters are numerous, further threatening an endangered wilderness. Now everything wild is threatened. Game and fur farms must replace hunting and trapping. Fishing continues to be fine today as long as done respectfully without catching too many. Most fish can also be farmed."

"You have saved us from tragedy," declared Cathy, "and shown us the beautiful side of what could be a harsh place."

"Respecting the wilderness is the way to enjoy it," stated Rin. "Too many people only enter the woods to kill something. When challenged they will say the kill is only part of the experience; but they would not go into the wilderness if there was to be no killing—and, for example, only pictures were to be taken. Hunting and trapping wild animals and birds should now be illegal because they have their own lives to live. They are not here to be shot. Farmed birds and animals are in a different situation because they are only present as they are raised for food."

"You don't just guide for fish," observed Cas.

"Maybe we should try to get some sleep," suggested Rin. "Tomorrow our journey south continues."

Dawn arrived bringing coolness to the forest. Rin, Cas, and Cathy walked, not just to continue their journey but also to stay warm. The terrain remained much the same with some areas of smooth rock, making progress pleasant, mixed with regions of forest and, hardest of all, watery areas that had to be crossed.

The night's camp brought warmth and dry clothes from a tall fire. Since there was no place to fish, the meal consisted of soup, tea, and biscuits. Exhaustion brought sleep early.

The next dawn was warmer, particularly when sunlight touched the travelers walking southward, following the shore. From the wilderness of water, trees, and rocks, there loomed the outline of a cottage.

"We should check and see if a door or window could be opened," suggested Rin. "Maybe inside, there would be a phone. We can leave a note outlining what we've had to do."

Finding a window open, Rin climbed inside then opened a door for Cas and Cathy. "There's a phone," he said. "I'm going to call the Coast Guard."

A phone call brought cheers at the Coast Guard office and sent a helicopter out to the cabin. Rin let Cas and Cathy tell their stories and these accounts became a legend that the new guy who had taken over the charter trips from Ben Canby was one of the best fishing guides in the north woods. This legend sent not only all Ben's customers but also many others to one known as the new guy.

People who owned the cabin, where the phone call to the Coast Guard had been made, were one of the first families to come to that region. They had started as commercial fishermen. After retiring from this occupation, they kept their cabin in the family as a cottage. They owned much land northward along the coast as well as inland. Rin bought some acres farthest from the cabin. He was able to purchase waterfront property in addition to land at the back leading to a small lake connected by a creek.

I've always wanted to build my own log cabin, he reflected while entering the office of an area builder. I don't have time now before winter. I'll have to hire a crew who build cabins. These people are known to be particularly good at working with logs.

"I hear you're the new guy with the big reputation who took over from Ben Canby," said a woman who sat behind a desk littered with papers. Notes also covered a wall behind her. Dark brown hair combed back into a ponytail, outlined a rounded face where fine features centered on her light brown eyes.

"I'm the new guy all right," agreed Rin. "I hear you are the very best at building log cabins."

"You hear correctly," she stated, smiling easily as a person who enjoyed meeting customers. "You have a cabin in mind?"

"If you have the time, I have the plans," he answered.

"I'm Sally—Sal—Crombie," she said. "And I have all the time you want to explain your plan."

"I'm the new guy," he replied. "Sometimes also known as Rin Fox."

"First time I've heard your actual name," she exclaimed. "Pleased to meet you both."

"Good to meet you," he added.

"Would you like coffee?" she asked.

"Thank you," he answered.

"Please sit down and prepare your information," she directed. "I'll get coffee. Black and no sugar?"

"Thank you," he replied.

"That's the woods-style, although many like to add sugar," she observed before standing and walking to a second table where she filled two mugs. Returning and placing one in front of Rin, she sat down and, smiling brightly, said, "Okay, let's hear what you would like—everything—all the details."

Rin proceeded to explain fully what he had dreamed into view while sitting in his room above the harbor. He had a deed, along with sketches, pictures, and maps outlining his plan's practical applications. Concluding he said, "I've also staked off the area, showing exact locations referred to here on paper."

"Perfect," she exclaimed. "Everything will go out on a barge. You'll be around also to answer questions and give directions?"

"Yes," he answered. "I'm available at my room above the harbor or at the site. I was going to build a cabin myself but could not outrun winter."

"Our crew will," she confirmed. "They'll live in tents and stay there until they've finished."

"You're as good as—even better than—your reputation," he stated.

"So are you," she added, smiling.

A few days later, Rin accompanied the barge and workboat carrying crew along with supplies to the cabin site. The boat that had sunk was insured. He had used insurance money to buy the new craft that he drove ahead of the builders to help show the route.

Arriving at his property, Rin recognized familiar landmarks of rocks where he had caught a large bass used to provide an outstanding meal for Casper and Cathy Woodstock. This fishing site was one of two rock outcroppings forming a channel into a small bay. The back shoreline was sandy with some stones. Farther back on an elevated plateau, there was a staked site for the new cabin.

After arriving on the shore, called the beach, the crew's foreman approached Rin. The foreman appeared to have natural leanness and strength. He had large hands and his handshake was strong. A lined leathery face was bordered by graying-brown hair and his eyes were gray. "Max Linton," said the guy.

"Rin—Rinton—Fox," replied Rin. "You didn't waste any time getting started on this project."

"Winter won't wait for us," Max stated. "Sal said you staked the site. I'll introduce the crew then maybe you could go over everything again with us. We like to get things right the first time."

"Good idea," noted Rin. "Maybe we could get started."

Walking with the foreman and crew, Rin proceeded to the site where he had previously put in stakes. He outlined markers at the four outer corners along with the stone fireplace on the west wall between two main windows. The south wall had a door and two windows in addition to being the site of the kitchen. At the back, or east wall, were two bedrooms, each with a window. Along the north wall were two windows and a door next to the bathroom. Out from this wall would be a propane fueled, freestanding fireplace. An upper story bedroom was also to be located above the other two bedrooms at the back, or east wall.

"I like your plan," concluded Max. "You've thought things through. The stakes beside the beach are for a dock where you will keep your boat?"

"Yes," Rin answered. "A pulley system will bring the boat up onto the beach for the winter. An outhouse would be built at the back of the cabin where there are four additional stakes. There will also be a well."

"We'll put up our tent, unload supplies, and get to work," concluded Max. "We are going to have some helpful weather for a while."

"I'm lucky to get you and your crew," noted Rin. "I thought of doing this work myself but winter is faster than I am."

"We'll be racing against the icing-over of your small bay," explained Max.

"If there's time, a shed by the water on the south side of the dock would be a good addition for the storage of a hovercraft," noted Rin.

"Between the solid ice of winter and open water, hover crafts are an increasingly popular form of transportation," added Max. "We'll include a shed. Maybe you could put in the stakes—and we'll get to work."

"I'll do the stakes right now," noted Rin before they both walked away to start their projects.

After marking a site for the shed, Rin returned to his boat and drove out through the rock channel. He turned northward to explore the shore, entering a region of rock, water, and pines where sunlight danced on a rippled surface of greenish-blue water and innumerable parts fit together to form magnificence Rin could watch and enjoy all day, every day and always see something new—a different blend of unparalleled beauty. Like the ocean, the water of Georgian Bay never rested and flowed in and out, always moving even when appearing to be calm.

While the cabin was being built, Rin continued to take clients sent to him by Ben Canby. Ben automatically sent his previous clients on to the new guy whose outstanding reputation had long ago become a legend. The tours were mainly for fishing yet also involved painting and filming.

Painting trips usually took place on islands where scenes for pictures were beyond any limits. During one photographic expedition, a client had just finished complaining "There's nothing here," when beside the boat the water's surface boiled upward before pouring away from the rising form of a massive bull moose with expansive antlers. The moose continued feeding on water lily roots while cameras caught one of the best sequences the complaining photographer had ever seen.

When Rin was not guiding other people, a favorite way of enjoying the wilderness was to sit down and remain motionless, or stretch out on a rock, and listen to the pure silence of the wild that once heard is addictive to the mind's seldom resolved quest for rest found in this case with the tonic of peacefulness.

CHAPTER SEVEN
THE CLIENT

When previous clients continued to contact Ben Canby, he told them to be at the main dock on a designated morning and he would have the new guy meet them there. To fulfill one of Ben's arrangements—the one most recently received—Rin Fox stirred in the darkness of morning then got up to greet the new day. He turned on a lamp that received electricity both from a solar panel on the roof and also a line strung on poles through the woods to the road that stopped at the last cottage whose owner had sold Rin the land.

Next Rin put on the propane fueled fireplace. It cast amber light through the new log structure with windows providing a view of the inlet and dock where the boat was tied.

He prepared breakfast consisting of the usual oatmeal porridge accompanied by toast topped with honey and jam. Lastly, there was coffee. Sipping the stimulating drink, he enjoyed the features of his cabin and looked forward to the new day. The weather was forecast to be excellent. Today's appointment was for fishing.

Without the aid of a flashlight, Rin left his cabin and walked to the boat, untied it then started the motor. First traces of dawn sufficiently outlined contours of a narrow passageway leading out of the inlet.

A light mist hung above the water. First light was distinctly outlining objects by the time Rin reached the main dock where the day's client waited and held a fishing pole.

Rin's skill brought the boat up to just nudge the dock where the customer stood. "Good morning," he greeted. "You're Ben Canby's previous client, Amber Rogers?"

"Yes," she answered. "Are you the new guy?"

"That's what they have started saying," he replied. "My name is Rin Fox."

"Rin Fox?" she gasped.

"Yes," he confirmed. "Didn't think there were many people with that name. You're Amber Rogers?"

"You're Rin Fox?" she almost screamed.

"Apparently," he confirmed, shocked by her reaction. Looking at her more closely, he said, "I've seen many amazing sights, most o' them recently, but very few, if any, like now. You're Amber Carlson. You changed your name?"

"Got married," she said softly, looking down. "Didn't last long. We're getting a divorce."

"The last time I saw you," he recalled, "you told me to go fishing. I might learn something. Well, I did go fishing. And I did learn something. You were right. I went fishing and learned many things, all beyond my wildest dreams."

"I can't believe it" she stated, her dark eyes fixed on him as though, if she looked away, he might vanish. "You're the new guy, a fishing guide—and a legend."

"Well," he said, as the situation started to envelop him, "I should say more probably but—at least—it's good to see you again."

"I should say it's good to see you again," she replied. "But you're not the person you were before. You're different. You are now what I thought I saw in you but you refused to recognize and I got fed up waiting. So I said, go fishing. You might learn something. You went fishing on a journey of no return. As I said, you've changed. You are now the person I saw in you originally. I hope the authentic you can accept me."

"I never rejected you," he stated. "Maybe we could go fishing. I have a story to tell you."

"A story I want to hear," she exclaimed.

After Rin started the motor, the first rays of sunlight lit up the boat, catching the craft in golden hues in addition to emblazoning surrounding mist where loons appeared. Two birds swam away from the advancing craft while their wild calls spoke to the awakening morning.

"I have a cabin to show you," said Rin while the boat moved through brightening mist.

"Along with the cabin," answered Amber, "I'd like to hear what happened to you after I told you to go fishing and sent you on a journey of no return. Our story is just beginning."

PART TWO

LOST
NO LONGER

CHAPTER ONE
THE HOLIDAY

A sleepless night started the journey. This should have come as a warning but was viewed with some accuracy as merely terrible preparation for each following occurrence. The driver of the van to the airport was knowledgeable about cocaine and each passenger was wiser at the departure. The airport itself presented a series of seemingly unending rules, checks, and lineups until there followed the longest delay of them all—waiting for departure.

In the airport, Benteen, or Ben Sands almost appeared to be just one of the crowd but he never could be entirely. Attention was not drawn to his height, as it was average like his generally strong appearance. Stature showed in his face where the jaw was strong, with high cheekbones. His grayish-brown hair did not stand out much but his eyes did. They were grayish-blue and indicated a person who missed little in the surrounding world.

The anticipated departure eventually arrived. Benteen felt the plane leave the runway and lift into a bank of clouds stacked upon each other and lit by lightning. Turbulence followed. Top racks almost emptied. Although not included in his previous plans, Ben purchased a beer then another. A third was attempted although not successfully.

The call that seemed would never come finally arrived when the flight attendant said, "Fasten your seat belts to prepare for landing."

A slight bump marked the plane's contact with the runway. The craft moved toward lights then stopped. Passengers started to unload luggage from overhead compartments.

Ben joined a file of people walking slowly along the aisle. Jubilation at the end of the flight was tempered by weariness. Checked baggage was secured before he rushed onward to rent a car.

At the service booth, his accumulation of fatigue helped the speed, if not accuracy, of answering questions while a business document was prepared. Paperwork having been completed, he walked to the parking lot where he selected a vehicle out of a choice of three.

With two travel bags in the back and rental documents topping the passenger seat, he drove out of the garage and followed lights bordering an access road leading to the main highway. Here he joined a stream of other vehicles visible mainly by lights. Lights imposed order to the night. Having the driver's side window down to catch fresh air, he felt relief in being able to finally take charge of the journey and not just be caught by it.

The world outside the vehicle changed little because most of it remained hidden by the murkiness of night. The noticeable parts, the lights, also started to vanish as apparently the countryside through which he was now traveling was less ordered by people.

Eventually, there remained only darkness lit by a path illuminated by his vehicle's headlights. The dark region became vast particularly after lights from other vehicles diminished then stopped. To fill the seemingly endless space of the night's realm, Ben started to add plans to support his dreams.

A loud bang coming from the front, driver's side of the car forced the steering wheel to lurch to the right. Ben threw all his strength into holding the wheel as the car bounced off the pavement. On the shoulder, he applied the brakes, sending the vehicle sliding to a stop.

Well at least I didn't hit anything, he said to himself as some of the cloud of dust around his car entered through the open window. A tire has blown and so has the start of my journey. According to my documents, I can call the listed number to get twenty-four-hour roadside assistance. And this I would do if I had a phone. I've joked about people always being on the phone and I'd never waste my time by getting one. That's another of my ideas that aren't always right. I'll put on emergency lights and see if I can get help. The lights were activated, sending out a distress signal yet no passing vehicles were present to see the message. That's the largest snake I've ever seen, he exclaimed to himself as a thick, slow, slithering reptile left the roadside and started winding its way across the pavement. I hope that thing keeps going. Shortly afterward, an alligator left foliage, where the snake had first appeared, and seemed to be following the reptile's trail. Well, thought Ben, I've seen an alligator hunting a python. I hope the hunter is successful although I could be considered to be prey by both of them.

When the scream of a large cat filled the night, Ben felt like the panther was screaming at him. He remained motionless although no other sounds followed except occasional splashes.

Lights appeared down the highway yet the approaching car did not stop. People are justifiably wary of getting involved, he reasoned, after the fourth vehicle sped past.

Out here in the dark on this roadside I suddenly realize I'm making a serious mistake, he concluded. Why am I waiting for the system to work? Like I fix my life myself, I'll fix this predicament on my own.

First, he located the spare tire and tools then jacked the car. After seeing the damaged tire move up off the roadside, he loosened the wheel and replaced it with the spare. Should've done that in the first place, he told himself after dropping the torn tire into the back. Next, he replaced the tools. I don't know why I delayed so long before I decided to look after the situation myself. Maybe I waited because at the car rental place there was formed the impression that money made the world go 'round—smoothly. I haven't previously relied on that system because I usually can't pay for it.

Now help arrives, he noted when a vehicle moved off the pavement and stopped behind the car. The truck was as derelict as the two wiry reprobates who stepped out of it. This vehicle was hardly roadworthy making a perfect match for the individuals themselves who apparently operated with a minimum of society's benefits. Thereby the men savored what little they received.

"Those donuts were nasty," said one who approached directly followed by the other. Their clothes were no cleaner than necessary and well worn. Both characters were lean, partially shaven with eyes that were dark and alert. "The coffee was fresh," continued the same man who stopped in front of Ben. "Need help?" the stranger asked.

"I did," answered Ben, wanting to get traveling again quickly. "I fixed it myself and am now leaving."

"We're happy to help," added the trailing man before he threw away an empty donut box. The lead guy walked back to their truck while Ben got into his vehicle. When he was reaching for the key, both intruders reappeared and each had a gun.

"We can't help you but you can help us," stated the leader. "Get out."

Ben slowly opened the door and stepped back on the roadside.

"Give me the keys," ordered the leader.

Ben followed this direction then the guy said, "All we want is cash—and the car."

When Ben didn't move the leader repeated, "The cash. This isn't our first go around."

Ben reached into a pocket containing the least amount of money then dropped some bills into the bandit's outstretched hand.

"You can leave now," said the guy. "You have some walking to do."

During the robbery, Ben considered each event, even the smallest, looking for an opening he could use to get control of this situation. Nothing appeared.

When the men were finishing their robbery, the leader said to the other, "We can't just leave him here. He'll bring trouble." An argument followed.

Touched by a cold shadow of warning, Ben realized death—his death—was being discussed. He left the roadside and was hurrying beyond some foliage when a shot slammed splinters of wood against the side of his face. He started running through thickets of vegetation while hearing the men pursuing him. Ben picked his way past trunks and branches, moving as swiftly as possible with his only thought now of keeping distance between himself and his death. Sounds of cracking branches and voices gradually became fainter and eventually vanished.

When only silence surrounded him, he stopped and sat down on a drooping branch of a massive live oak. Looking up past a network of branches, draped with moss, he enjoyed one of few openings to a pale sky. Aside from the sky, observed Ben, there is only one other light brightening the foliage and in the morning I'll walk toward this light. Maybe there'll be a house.

Resting on the branch, leaning his back on the upward curve, he let exhaustion overtake him. I set out on this journey, he reflected, because I needed a holiday. So far, however, this situation seems to be a long way from the holiday I expected. I knew I needed a break when I had to drink coffee to stay awake during the meetings that I, as store manager, was supposed to be directing. At these occasions, the same people seemed to get importance in life, not through honest work, but in being heard, as if at such times they reached their heights of achievement not by what was said but in the fact they were speaking and others were supposed to be listening. I usually wasn't. When someone was talking, I was more and more often dreaming about what else I would like to do. I've always been in a hurry even when there seemed to be no obvious reason for rushing other than being pushed by a nagging awareness that life was short and should never be wasted. I wanted not just to get by but to make something, achieve something. In our business, success was measured financially. Our margin of profit on grocery items was small. Numerous sales kept us in business and volume was difficult to grow. We seemed to get the same section of customers regardless of what sparkle was added to the bait. Loss leaders—taking a loss on one item to get people into the store—too often ended in too much of a loss. I also like to help people and would do more if our store could afford more. Our dollar a turkey offer at Christmas is a loss commercially although provides a lot of happiness.

A grunt startled Ben. Suddenly he again felt fatigued—along with thirst and hunger. Another grunt followed by a snort brought his attention to a rustling clump of bushes. Lastly, he saw the deadly tusks, snout, and small eyes as a boar stepped away from the brush. Every muscle in the lean body seemed tense in anticipation of battle. The pig charged with unexpected speed and almost caught Ben. He missed the tusks by climbing higher along the sloping branch. After breaking off a section of dead wood, he returned. Mustering all his strength, he swung his new weapon, slamming it down on the attacker's head. The animal was too dazed to avoid the next blow or those that followed.

Well, thought Ben, after he sat down. That pig set out to kill something and was successful. I'll be successful too if I can prepare roast pork. First, I'll have to make a knife.

He searched the area until he located a section of coral beside a stream. After dislodging a heavy chunk, he used it to hammer the two tusks. Both not only dislodged but also cracked. Honing followed until two large splits became knives and four smaller pieces formed spear points. The pieces were worked steadily to add sharp edges to the implements. Lastly, the knives cut pork steaks.

After returning to the stream, he followed its bank until he located oyster shells and selected the best two. One provided a sharp cutting edge for a knife and the second served as an ax blade. Strips of pig hide secured handles to knives along with shafts for the spear points.

Having worked himself into a state of sweaty exhaustion, he risked drinking from the creek before washing both himself and his clothes. He hung clothes on shrubs to dry.

While sitting on the live oak branch, he concluded, it's a good thing I've always been a worker. Being a grocery store manager also helps because I've had to take charge and be self-reliant in order to find solutions to an almost endless variety of dilemmas. Importantly, however, I'll have to make a source of friction in order to get fire for cooking. If I could make containers, I would definitely boil water before drinking it. To get a spark, I'll rub pieces of wood together. I could twirl wood rapidly by first making a bow drill.

Benteen cut a long strip of pig hide then rolled it into a cord. He bent a piece of branch and tied it in a bow using the cord. Before being secured to each end of the bow, the cord was first looped around a shaft of hard, dry wood. He braced the shaft's upper end with an indented chunk of wood to protect his left hand. When his right hand moved the bow back and forth the vertical shaft rotated swiftly. Its lower end lodged into another piece of dry hard wood forming a base.

Satisfied with his work, he sat down on the branch and reassessed his situation. The friction of the rotating shaft against the base should create a spark, he concluded. A few dry shavings would ignite and I'll have a fire. I'll cut longer cords from the hide because I'll need snares and fish line. Tonight I'll watch for that light, fix its location then I'll walk that way and hopefully find people—with a house and road. I know the sun rises in the east and sets in the west. When I was rushing through brush my purpose was to escape from the two scavengers. I didn't think about where the road was located until I had no way of knowing. That's happened to me so often in life. If I'd only look ahead—plan for the future. During my earlier years, I had a chance to buy real estate when it wasn't expensive. Now that I'm aware of its financial value other people have also seen land's potential and put prices beyond my reach. When I could have remembered the location of the road, my attention was on other things that at the time were considered to be more urgent. Both topics were urgent. I must plan ahead. I should be aware of the directions and know what is located at the end of each route. Now I'm lost but I'll mark the light tonight.

After assembling fire-starting materials, Ben built a place where a fire could burn without harming surrounding trees or brush. For igniting materials he selected a dry, abandoned bird's nest. Lastly, he used the bow to rotate a vertical shaft. He kept at this task until a spark appeared. A flame started but extinguished when more dry materials were added.

The first flame was encouragement. Four flames later he managed to coax a tendril from shavings to swarm and grow among larger chunks until there was established a steadily burning fire. Now, exclaimed Ben to himself, I can sit down on this trunk and enjoy the comforts of a fine fire.

Life has always been hard for me, he mused. Maybe that's why I'm coping—so far successfully—with this ordeal. Necessity has pushed me beyond the debilitating tentacles of worry. I don't have the luxury—the time—to worry. As with the situation at the car, I had to act or die. I could not attack them because they each had a gun and one good shot was all they needed. Seemed to be more sensible to walk away when they were making plans. All three of us were improvising. The two scavengers could not have had the robbery planned although they seemed experienced in the lifestyle. They were small-timers but just as potentially deadly as any of the better-known dangers like the infamous cottonmouths or rattlesnakes.

I have saved meat from the hog, noted Ben after wrapping steaks in leaves. Now I'll have to move camp because other residents would be after the remainder of this food. The most logical place to stay would be close to the stream.

He followed the rivulet downstream until he saw another massive, live oak. Here he prepared a base for a fire then returned to his first fire for coals. In a short time, another flame was burning steadily. After moving the rest of his few supplies, he extinguished the first fire.

Again I feel exhausted, he exclaimed to himself after washing in the creek. The water not only cleans my skin and clothes but also revives my tired spirit, leaving me refreshed and maybe somewhat optimistic.

Along with taking some money and car, the bandits stole my planned holiday—not that I had much scheduled. They weren't skilled thieves, being more like bandits of opportunity. They missed most of my money that I never carry all in one place and they didn't even look for my credit card. Maybe they knew any purchases logged would provide a trail to be followed. The car and noticeable cash were opportunities in abundance particularly when life is lived with small expectations and minimal efforts. The men were finishing coffee and donuts and likely such extravagances had taken all remaining money. I presented the next payroll.

I've lost a rental car, some cash, and a planned holiday, he observed after adding more dry wood to the flame. Next to it, he had driven two forked stakes. Across the forks, a skewer held a slice of pork. Fat sizzled as it dripped into flames. Normally I don't cook pork because, like bear's meat, there are ailments present that can be passed on to people. Some individuals who have eaten this food without cooking it sufficiently have become very sick. My new supply of pork could contain a record number of unexpected surprises. Accordingly, I'll add extra cooking time to ensure any steaks roasted over one of my fires will have no survivors other than myself. I always liked the aroma of frying bacon, the scent of wood smoke, and along with the flavor of baked beans, these things remind me of tents and wild places. I used to enjoy such adventures until I started putting too much of my time into the grocery business. Years of work at least provided me with financial resources. Oh, but I paid for them. I'm reminded of the Indigenous leaders commenting on benefits received from land transactions when there was said something like, "We do not thank you for our rights because we paid for them and the price we paid was exorbitant."

I'd better pay attention to my cooking, Ben reminded himself. I no longer smell the tantalizing aroma of frying bacon. My steaks have advanced into the realm of burnt meat.

Using the skewers to hold the steak, Ben started having his first meal since getting lost. His hunger said the steak was delicious. After finishing the food, he enjoyed a drink from the stream. I've been too busy to check the sun, he noted, but I now see that sunset was long enough ago to have erased all colors from the sky except shades of night.

When an owl hooted to greet the night before starting to hunt, Ben thought of an owl as company. I've always enjoyed their calls and presence. Crows start a ruckus when they spot an owl. I also like crows— and all birds except those, such as hawks, that kill others. Starlings, blue jays, and crows raid bird's nests. I overlook the night work done by owls.

Time to sleep, he concluded before climbing to the place where his massive branch joined the trunk. He relaxed for the first time in a long time. Much later he drifted into the restfulness of deep sleep.

He was awakened at dawn by a clamor of crows disturbing an owl farther up in the live oak. How could I be so careless? he asked himself. I forgot to watch for the light. Maybe it's still visible. He searched each direction until, feeling a flood of relief, he thought—was sure—there was light. He noted its direction in relation to the brightening area where the sun would rise.

I'll cook another meal then follow this light. It seems to be different from the one I saw previously but dawn's brightness would change the appearance of landmarks. The stream flows toward the light. This creek will be my guide along with my source of fresh water.

Benteen traveled all day although nothing seemed to change. He almost expected to see his old camp appear again. There was no camp, however. A new stopping place had to be assembled. This time he had advantages. Coals from the other fire, wrapped with moss then leaves, soon ignited sending a flame climbing along dry kindling. Larger pieces of wood were added and in a short time a new flame burned steadily. Above this heat, a pork steak roasted. When a tantalizing fragrance of frying bacon soured with a stench of burned meat, Ben started his meal.

The food was improved with the addition of a salad made by first chopping with the oyster hatchet then boar's tusk knife to uncover the center of a young cabbage palm. The cabbage palm lived up to its name and helps to improve meals here in the swamp, observed Ben as he saved large chunks for future meals. The palm should remain fresh for a long time but the pork will soon spoil, he warned himself. I must dry and smoke some of it.

After building a drying rack above the fire, he topped the pole frame with pieces of pork. Leaves added to the fire supplied extra smoke to help preserve the meat.

Feeling weary after the smoking process, he removed most of his clothes then washed them in the creek. Lastly, he stretched out in the water leaving only his chest and face above the surface. The movement of flowing water had a soothing, restful impact. He looked up beyond foliage to the night sky sprinkled with stars.

The stars remind me I did not see the light amid foliage tonight, he recalled. I know the direction where the light appeared and this creek is flowing the way I want to travel. I don't like to admit it, but maybe I might be enjoying this experience. It isn't anything I planned and I would always try to avoid such a predicament. Now that I'm here, lost in unknown terrain, I'm finding the experience to be an interesting challenge. The largest events of my life are those I did not see coming— like this situation. Maybe—likely—it's not what happens to us that is the main concern. The important aspect of life is the way we react to what takes place. God does not throw us into difficulties. It is amazing to consider—since life is forever—we plan obstacles ourselves before we come here from the spiritual side in order to experience and thereby discover what we came here to learn. Anyone can react well to good times. Tests come with hard knocks. And difficulties we would all prefer to avoid. Wouldn't it shock us if we were to discover—as I now think—that we are here for the hard knocks? Not that we do harm on purpose but just being a resident on earth is trouble and that's why we come here to experience and learn what can't be determined in the spiritual home of the other side where there is no trouble.

"Ahhhh," screamed Ben as something slithered across his face and chest. He scrambled out of the water, stood on the bank, and looked downstream to see what had slithered past. Turning toward him was a large snake. Its mouth opened flashing a white interior and Ben whispered, "The thing's a water moccasin—a cottonmouth. Instead of watching stars and dreaming, I'd better be more aware of my surroundings."

He located the comfortable curve where his branch joined the main trunk and slept soundly until the dawn. After gathering his small assortment of supplies, he snacked on some pork along with cabbage palm then resumed his journey.

The brush was particularly thick containing an abundance of saw palmettos. While pressing onward, his clothes got ripped. I must look as wild as this landscape, he noted during one of his occasional stops to rest beside the stream. Maybe other predators will see me coming and run in panic. So far though that hasn't been happening. I don't like the way alligators eye me. They are a constant menace along with large rattlesnakes. All these potentially aggressive creatures have shown little reaction to me, indicating that I'm likely the first person they've encountered. If they had previous experience, I suspect they would react violently to my presence either fearing me or seeing me as being something easy to catch. I don't see them as good to eat. The only food possibilities I've noticed—other than pork—are frog legs. They can be found on menus in the best seafood restaurants. I think I'll put frog legs on the menu in this "live with the food and try not to be part of the food" restaurant. Bullfrogs in here are huge and have legs almost comparable to chickens.

At first hearing thrashing sounds then seeing the open jaws of a charging alligator, Ben ran with more speed than he thought he possessed. Knowing a gator at a full charge could outrun him he sought refuge on the limb of a vine-wrapped live oak.

He was just beginning to relax when he noticed the largest vine start to move. One end of it took the shape of a python's head. It was approaching.

Ben slammed his spear through the creature, impaling it just behind the head. The serpent writhed into a bundle, losing its grip on the trunk and dropping to the ground where the gator struck it immediately.

By the time the sun started descending behind clouds, turning them to crimson, the alligator walked away with the remaining portion of snake dragging behind like a packed lunch. Better the snake than me being on that guy's menu, thought Benteen as he watched one predator drag the other away. I've had enough ground level for one day. I think I'll stay here and leave in the morning.

The night was uneventful aside from a nightmare when he had to fight off a giant snake and almost fell off the branch. I was in one nightmare and woke up to another he noted when he recognized his surroundings. More fitful sleep followed before he could welcome the dawn.

The rising sun found him more worried than usual. Warm rays brightening his watery, humid surroundings could not dispel a chill in his spirit or grayness clouding the way he now saw his situation. The light has gone, he told himself. Why would it come and go? Maybe it's a good sign—that people are active ahead. Or has the winding course of the creek lost the strand of hope I've been grasping? I'll continue following the route I've established. To do otherwise is to risk losing my way again. At least now I have a plan. Getting lost once should be enough at one time.

Ben kept traveling while a blend of days and nights joined to become lost to any concept of marking time's passage. His journey continued until a seemingly endless tangle of foliage, trunks and moss started to clear ahead. Maybe I'm approaching a vast swamp, he warned himself. I'll have to stay optimistic and not face obstacles until I see them. The real dangers here are enough and I can only hope they aren't too overwhelming. I have to believe I'll solve this dilemma. I've enough obstacles. If I become one myself, I don't have a chance. Maybe that's the difference between good failure and devastation. Good failure leads us back to our true-life course. Failure of devastation occurs when we reach an obstacle offering an opportunity to enhance our life; but rather than select such a successful path, we turn away from our highest potential and choose to quit. That's the failure of devastation.

Keeping himself company with his thoughts, he kept walking until he stopped, stood, and stared in disbelief. He could walk no farther. Ahead stretched a seemingly endless expanse of water. "I'm at the Gulf of Mexico," he shouted, although his words were absorbed by open space. "The surface is likely as calm as the Gulf gets with only a slight lap of water against mangroves bordering the shore. The light that gave me direction did not come from a cabin," he shouted, finding some comfort in hearing the company of his own words. "My beacon must have come from a boat. This is a mangrove-bordered cove. Vessels might anchor out but would have no reason to come in. I'm going to take a chance with a choice of direction and follow the left shore. Sometime—someday—I should reach a building. In this area, storms could get particularly severe, including water surges. I should travel with lots o' caution."

Benteen pushed onward, attempting to follow the coast. The Gulf was always kept in sight although it was sometimes only a distant glimmer guarded by long stretches of mangroves. His shoes had to be tied on to at least cover the bottoms of his feet. Trousers became shorts while shirts were minimal barriers to the sun. Material from a shirt covered the top of his head. His hair gradually became long and shaggy like his beard. After starting with pork, meals consisted of roasted fish, frog legs, or oysters along with cabbage palms.

He stopped and stared in disbelief when he saw orange trees. How would they get here? he asked himself. I won't question good fortune. I need juice and vitamins. With shaking hands, he ravenously peeled an orange and, like a person in a desert finding a well, he savored the juice and its sweet taste. With juice running down his chin, he finished one then another, continuing until he was beyond full.

I might have to build a shelter here because I'm always in need of something to drink. Juice provides a constant supply. After resting, I could carry oranges with me and keep traveling. First, however, I'll look for a good place to build a shelter and also see if I can discover how orange trees came to be planted here.

The question of how orange trees arrived was solved when he noticed the outline of a square marked in the ground. A settler's cabin, he exclaimed. Possibly one of the first European settlers stayed here.

There's a freshwater creek. They must've had some way to boil water for purification and cooking.

Using a stick, he dug along the inside of the square hoping to find some utensils that had not rotted. Like a person uncovering a life raft, he uncovered the side of a rounded object. Frantic digging brought into his trembling hands a precious, copper pot. Further work dislodged a copper container with line and hooks of the same material. "What a discovery," he shouted. These items would be some of the settler's prized possessions—at least those that have not disintegrated. A dislodged, pottery cup sent his hopes soaring again until the prize fell into two pieces. A second cup did not break. "What gifts," he shouted again. I was really living at the slimmest edge of survival until I came here, he admitted to himself after he sat down to stop trembling. I can now boil water for drinking and variation in food. The fishing line will add to spearing.

A search of the cabin site continued. After a few days of work, his life was further assisted by the recovery of a rusted knife and ax head. He honed these tools with a piece of coral until workable sharpness resulted.

Selecting a site close to the Gulf where he could watch for boats, he started building his first really adequate shelter. Poles imbedded vertically in sand kept the floor of the structure above the ground for protection. On this elevated base, walls were added then topped by a roof covered with overlapping palmetto leaves. A sleeping area was made more comfortable by chinking moss between floor poles. Walls were also chinked. In front of the structure, he built a comfortable chair and a fire pit where he kept a fire burning on sand encircled by coral rocks. Lastly, the interior of his new home received two more chairs along with a table.

The first occupants were much smaller than the builder. They were lizards and many of them. They provided pleasant company when Ben sat inside his completed shelter. It faced the Gulf and a strip of sand where waves almost always splashed onto the shore. Lights appeared occasionally from boats far out in the Gulf. None—or few—came near shore likely because the small strip of sand would be unnoticed from any distance in the generally inhospitable coastal area.

Testing the shelter, a storm hit the region. The setting sun vanished behind fast-moving, black clouds that brought rain-filled wind to thrash the land and shake the new structure. Its roof held and kept out water that found revenge in spraying between openings in walls.

The next day brought the usual heat. This time of year, noted Ben when he awakened amid first light as it returned to help erase any remnants of the storm, the best time to work or travel is at first light in the morning or last light in the evening. Early and late are the times to find refreshing coolness. The middle of the day belongs to full sunlight and its heat. There's also humidity. An almost constant breeze from the Gulf brings a refreshing movement of air. This morning, I'll try out the copper line and hooks. First, though I'm going to need a sinker. After locating a piece of coral with a hole in it, he tied this weight to the end of the line. Up a few feet, he tied a hook.

At the water's edge, he hurled his spear into a school of minnows splashing at the surface. Two scaled sardines, or greenbacks, were injured. He caught them, hooked one on the line then let the coil release as the sinker was tossed out to deeper water.

With the line in place, he sat down on a ridge of sand and waited while, through a cloud-strewn sky, an eagle soared. Sunlight danced on waves cresting before breaking in a song that Ben found to be the most peaceful music he had ever heard.

I thought of this admission earlier, he recalled, but I like to search deeply rather than just act by letting each event progress to the next without full prior consideration. However, I have to admit getting rescued is no longer my purpose if that ever was my intent except at first when I was robbed and forced to escape. My car rental company might consider me to be a thief unless the two scavengers abandoned the vehicle, knowing the police would be looking for it. The men seemed to be two derelicts just surviving from day to day. Coffee and donuts recently purchased probably represented a high point of special treats and might have taken a large part or all the remaining money. Such characters were too poor to be part of any larger, criminal organization. Like the donuts and coffee that were momentary highlights the car would be the same and would be discarded along the roadside. I will be at first listed as missing. Now I'm probably presumed to be dead.

A strike on the bait caught Ben by surprise and almost jerked the line from his hands. He pulled back to set the hook then worked with the catch, releasing line at the height of each thrust before retrieving some whenever possible. Gradually loops reformed in his left hand while to shore and upon the sand there came a silvery-blue and turquoise-hued Spanish mackerel. There were marks of gold on the fish's sides.

A wonderful catch, declared Ben while he carried his prize toward the fire. After the mackerel had stopped struggling, it was prepared on a spit above the fire. The fish cooked quickly, turning to moist, white meat accompanied by an orange for its juice.

I don't think a better meal could be obtained at any restaurant, he noted after finishing the food then resting on his outside chair. When I was at work and attending those seemingly endless meetings, life was not even close to being as rich as this experience. The meetings seemed to be only an attempt to persuade everyone that work was being achieved in lives that had little other evidence of accomplishment other than daily routines providing structure like walls support a building. Beyond a veil of illusions and pretenses, money was the real purpose. I have money now, that the thieves did not find, and it's of no value to me because here I'm in the midst of real-life where diligence brings the payment of another day and carelessness results in an end to life. The more fully and wisely life is met the greater is the chance for survival. If I had bemoaned my lot, became depressed, and waited to be rescued, I would be dead just as the world I left now considers me to be. If I had panicked and run amuck, I would've met the same fate. Although I haven't thought this through previously, I'm now sure it's not what happens to us that counts, it's what we do in response that writes the story for each life. And there's no substitute for hard work and thinking things through before going to work. After something has happened, following the right path afterward is essential to surviving and proceeding to the next obstacle. Cheating the life experience by not following your trail to improvement but looking for what seems the easiest way and stealing rewards that come from another's work brings only the outward appearance of productivity while the place where everything is tested—in the spirit—remains untried, empty and dark. People, not the Creator, make their own hell. I've thought of this here because in such a wild place I've discovered not an empty realm that is valueless until exploited but a garden of timeless, created life that is destroyed when exploited by land developers, oil companies, or other miners who see no treasure until the environment is boiled down to oil, logs or other products. The true value of this land, like all regions, exists before the developers arrive. Resources are needed although their extraction must not destroy the source of supply. In this undeveloped region, I have found life. An abundance of creatures live in a balance that has survived through ages because here there is the timeless quality of life. The product left behind here is life in abundance. Too often the product left behind by an oil company, logger, or other land developer is destruction and death such as in the examples of bitumen and fracked gas. During my present journey, I've found natural, wilderness life and this has enriched my life. I feel part of this wilderness and that must explain why the more I've been out here the less I feel alone because every day I've been more naturally connected to the Creator. I previously went to the Christian church as other people go to churches of their choice. I now realize the important part is in striving to stay with the Creator and not turn away. Those who turn away make their own darkness or hell. In this place, I've found life and each day I feel less and less urgency to leave. I see as outsiders the boats moving past along the Gulf. I feel no desire to return. Someday I will go back but I now know I'll never really leave but will always come home where there is the spirit and that's all that matters. I have money and haven't needed it because here there is life. Money is not the currency of life. Money buys useful products but it is useless without a spiritual life. I'll always be grateful for those two crooks because they gave me disastrous trouble. What counts is not what happens to us. Only the choices we make afterward matter and that's the purpose of our life journey—realizing what we can't learn in our spirit home where there's no trouble. We come from our spiritual home and we'll go back there if we don't turn away. Wilderness is the purest beauty of the spiritual world. I've found it here, seen it, and will never be the same again.

When I first got here, thought Ben while he continued to be caught up in understanding all that had happened, I was lost. I've journeyed a lifetime and I'm lost no longer. When I have the chance, I'll try to get other people to meet the wilderness where they can see life in order to better know, find, and experience their lives. I'll be a guide. That's the work I'll do now. I'll guide others to the life I've discovered. I'll take them to the wilderness so they can have an opportunity to see it. Their journeys can't be rushed as each person will travel at his or her own speed and will be using individual maps.

Distracted from his thoughts by a boat passing at the usual distance far off the coast, Ben decided, I could stay in this wilderness forever. There are people around although they seem to miss this stretch of shore. They drive past always in a hurry to get somewhere else. Although I'm content to remain like the settlers who probably lived all their lives around this cabin, I should at least for a while return to the outside world.

The next day the first light of dawn found Ben leaving his camp and taking one last look back. Finally turning around, he resumed walking, attempting to follow the shoreline. Waves rolling onto sand provided him with a traveling companion. Caught by this peaceful sound, I can walk particularly long distances, he reflected just before he saw the mangrove-bordered inlet ahead. These places are the hardest obstacles to cross, he recalled. Not only is there varying depth of water but also brush adds concealment for snakes and alligators.

Speaking of gators, he warned himself when he saw the eyes, I must proceed more cautiously. A manatee surfaced for a gulp of air then submerged leaving behind a few ripples. An osprey flew overhead. An American egret resting on a branch watched as Ben reached shallow water leading to a stretch of shore comprised of shell sand.

He walked onward until, in a particularly open area, he was startled by the sudden intrusion of the outside world. It had been passing in the distance and now, like a foreign, out-of-place, unwelcome intruder, a small boat with a motor was pulled up against a strip of sand where a man and woman were resting on blankets and sharing a bottle of wine.

Ben fought away a feeling that they did not belong and were trespassing. I guess I'm the one who has been away and have now been confronted—attacked—by a world that I thought I'd left behind, he reasoned. I suppose I must someday reconnect although I'm not sure I want to.

A loud, piercing scream froze Ben's thoughts. The woman stared at him, stood up and the man followed. She rushed to the boat, got into it, sat down at the back then started working with the motor. As the man hurried to keep up with her he kept one hand pointed at Ben.

Shocked by this reaction, Ben shouted, "I'm friendly."

Keeping his hand pointed, the man replied, "We're not."

Ben realized the pointed hand held a gun as the guy stepped inside the boat. He sat down just before the woman started the motor. The craft sped toward a larger craft anchored offshore. The man and woman were soon aboard the larger vessel and it returned to become just another boat passing off the coast.

Ben walked to the place where the two people had been resting. On the sand, there was a pack of cigarettes topped by a lighter. Like a man finding a treasure, Ben picked up the lighter, snapped on its flame, and saw his life get easier.

Strange, how those people reacted, he thought as he resumed his journey. I might have been shot. They were the intruders. Such arrogance. I can understand better now why Indigenous people are outraged and insulted when their homelands not only get occupied but the invaders claim the original owners don't belong here. Visitors come from distant places and think they, the intruders, own the land. Then they cut it to pieces to get what is deemed more valuable than the unlimited treasure and life-giving home of the land itself. This situation is difficult to understand—but now I see the absurdity. I might have been shot and they would've said they were only defending themselves. Such arrogance.

Ben kept walking. While he traveled, the number of boats he saw increased. Added to these occasional sightings, there arrived a more constant stench of fumes and drone of motors to break the peace of silence or overlap sounds of waves and calls of birds.

I don't see these natural areas as waste territory, noted Ben after he once again thought of the two intruders on the beach. They treated me as an intruder into their world. I saw them as they saw me.

That night the new lighter helped to grill a meal of red drum or redfish. Food brought little comfort. Ben was saddened, knowing he was starting to walk out of the region that had become his home. Wilderness continues to live in many areas, he told himself. Also, there are pockets of the wild like the one where I've been living. While there is wilderness, the true beauty of the natural world will live where people can continue to bask in its infinite beauty and knowledge. I can always come back to renew my spirit.

A few days later Ben was crossing another section of mangroves when he heard not only boats and but also cars along with people's voices. Going to seem strange to talk again with people, he cautioned himself. The shock of adjusting to the life I left behind is going to be as great as the challenge I previously experienced learning to live in the natural world that has now become my home.

He stepped out of the water and started climbing an embankment comprised of shell sand and coral dumped to cover a large section of a mangrove bay. At the top, cars were parked beside a bar located next to a beach. The bar was part of a business named the *End of the Road Beach Resort*.

Hesitating at first, Ben strode to the bar, opened its front door then entered a large, dimly lit room. Windows were open and waves could be heard splashing along the sand.

Interior air stank of alcohol. A murmur of people talking vanished leaving behind an empty silence broken only by the muffled sound of customers moving away from where Ben was standing. Nearby tables were vacated along with an adjacent stretch of the bar. Ben walked to this area and sat down on a stool closest to the door.

Behind the opposite end of this long, curving counter, there stood a bartender. He had long, straight, dark hair, and a similar beard bordering a narrow, pensive face lit by dark eyes. Appearing to be a person who did nothing swiftly and jumped to no conclusions, he stroked his beard with his right hand as if anything he might say would come out of deep thought. He wore a loose-fitting white Tee shirt matched by similar fitting faded jeans, as if these items made up his working uniform. Both shirt and jeans covered a narrow frame. He had stopped what he had been doing, straightened to his full height, and considered the person who had just sat down on the far bar stool. The other customers had made their decisions about this new guy because the others had vacated the entire surrounding area.

The bartender continued to stroke his beard pensively, always thinking before acting. The sight before him was something new to his bar. The visitor had remnants of sandals tied to his feet. He wore shorts consisting of wound material and leather cords holding rudimentary tools including a roughly hewn hatchet and knife together with a pot and cup. The man's right hand held a spear. Its white point was kept in place by a tightly tied leather strip.

The visitor was lean along with being well muscled. His hair and beard were long and tangled in addition to being a mixture of gray and brown. Eyes peering out through this foliage were grayish-blue with an alertness indicating a person who missed little in his surroundings. The face displayed a stature with a strong jaw and high cheekbones.

Stepping forward, the bartender, speaking softly, asked, "Gone back to the land?"

"Not by choice at first," Ben answered. "Choice came later."

"I'm a bit surprised to hear you speak," said the bartender.

"I'm a bit surprised to hear you speak," countered Ben.

"Don't get many homeless people in here," continued the bartender.

"I'm not homeless," explained Ben. "I can live anywhere—in the wilderness."

"Were you goin' to order something?" asked the proprietor again.

"Yes," came the reply.

"Will you be a paying customer?" came the next question.

"Yes," said Ben.

"What would you be ordering?" he asked.

"Let's start with draft beer followed by the special you have listed then a cup of coffee and a glass of clean water," replied the guy with the spear as if such customers came into the bar all the time.

"Okay," said the bartender before he walked away to place the order then pour a glass of draft. Returning and placing a tall glass of beer in front of this wild man, the bartender asked, "How long have you been homeless—living anywhere?"

"Since I got robbed by two scrawny guys driving a beat-up, old truck," answered Ben. "When they were arguing about killing me, I took cover in adjacent foliage and a shot just missed my head. I moved fast—lost them and got lost myself. I've been living in the wilds ever since."

"Where'd you get the pot and cup?" enquired the bartender.

"Found them at an old settler's cabin," Ben answered.

"How long have you been out there?" the bartender asked again.

"I'm not sure," he replied.

"What's your name?" continued the bartender.

"Benteen Sands," he answered.

"I'm Chuck Canby," he said. "Pleased to meet you," he added before they shook hands. Turning to walk away, the proprietor said, "Be right back." He hurried to the far end of the bar where there was a phone. After dialing a number, he waited before asking, "Cal? Chuck. Drop what you're doing and get down here. I've got a story for you. You'll never get a better one. Don't wait."

Returning to find the customer savoring the cool drink, Chuck stated, "Been a long time."

"Yup," exclaimed the wild-looking customer. "There were a few luxuries I did not have in the bush. I gotta say though I found more deeply restful peace in the wilderness than I find on the outside. Between my two lives, I'd pick the wilderness. We've gained luxuries on the outside. The essentials though I found in the wilds. In acquiring the extras in life we so often overlook or even lose life itself. I left stress and work behind to go on a holiday where I found not only peace and quiet but also life itself. I'll go back every chance I get. Should I ask whom you called?"

"A reporter," answered Chuck stroking his beard. "She used to work for the New York Times. Came out to this area in search of where her ancestors had settled when they arrived here in 1850. She checks every story. Has written many good accounts for local newspapers. So far has found nothing about her family. Her name's Calley, or Cal Nelson."

Chuck walked back to the kitchen where, on a counter, there rested the ordered special—chili, fish chowder, and coffee.

When the food was placed in front of Ben, he exclaimed, "Good to have a change—although meals were fine where I've been. While I'm experiencing this change in diet, would you please make another call? Call the police."

"You sure you want me to do that?" asked Chuck. "You definitely aren't my average wild-looking customer. Usually, I'm the one callin' the police—not the wild customers."

"I'm sure," he confirmed. "Later I'll contact the car rental company—but I should check in with the police first. Likely they've looked for me and unofficially think I'm dead."

Walking back to the phone, Chuck turned and asked, "You're positive about this?"

"Yes," he replied. "Thanks for making the call."

While savoring the food, Ben heard Chuck say, "Have you been looking for Benteen Sands? Well, he just asked me to call you. Yeah, that's me. I'm sober. He looks very much alive to me. Right now he's enjoying our special. He looks as wild as they come but talks like a regular person. Said two guys driving an old truck stopped and robbed him when he was fixing a flat tire. They were discussing killing him so he took cover in roadside brush. They shot at him but he kept running, got lost, and just now stepped out of the wild—although he still looks wild."

When Chuck left the phone and approached his customer, Ben said, "Thanks for calling. I had to check in with them and let them know I'm not dead."

"She thought the call was a hoax at first," confirmed Chuck. "Asked me if I was sober."

"I heard," observed Ben.

"Unofficially they thought you'd be dead," continued Chuck.

"Stands to reason one would be deceased who has been missing in such country for so long," noted Ben. "I hope she wasn't disappointed. I probably changed all of her neatly filed paperwork."

"She took the news well," added Chuck. "Actually she was shocked. "A car will probably be arriving soon."

Ben finished the meal while Chuck helped other customers. Looking out a window, he said, "The reporter's here now."

Entering the bar, Calley appeared to be a person who not only had beauty but did not seem to be aware of it—as though it was there although a story—possibly the story of her career—was all she was lit up about. Medium length brown hair tied at the back was swept away from a narrow face where pale brown eyes displayed enjoyment of life along with a depth of character in a person who looked for the roots of a story and not just appearances.

Stopping in her tracks when she saw Ben, as he was clearly more than anything she had anticipated, she composed herself, smiled brightly, and asked, "Okay Chuck, where's the story?"

Laughing, he replied, "The customer at the far end of the bar."

Pointing, she asked, "That the one?"

"Yes," he replied, laughing again.

Turning to Ben, she said, "Apparently you're the one I've come to interview. Do you mind if I ask you some questions?"

"I'm Ben—Benteen Sands," he replied.

She shook hands with him, saying, Cal—Calley Nelson. Reporter. If you don't mind I'd like to do a story about you."

"Well it's quite a story and telling it is fine with me," he answered.

"I see you found a pottery cup," she noted.

"Yes," he confirmed.

"Can I?" she asked, walking toward the cup and reaching for it.

"Of course," he said before she held it then examined each part.

Calley's scream startled Ben and Chuck along with bringing renewed silence and turning heads in the rest of the room.

"What the..." gasped Ben while Chuck stroked his beard.

Holding the upturned cup in her hands and pointing to the bottom, she declared in a strained voice, "There are indented the initials W M N. They're the initials of my great grandmother, Winnifred McCord Nelson. She was from Scotland. In England, she married Charles Nelson. They came to America and settled along this shore in 1850. They traded with the Seminoles who were separatists from the Creeks farther north mainly in Alabama. I have read records and my great grandparents were particularly friends with one family, the Panthers. After the deaths of Winnifred and Charles, their son and daughter eventually settled on the prairie across the Canadian side. From there, members of the family moved eastward to Ontario. I'm a reporter and came south basically in a search for my great grand-parents settlement. Up till now, I've found little evidence of where they actually settled."

Directly to Ben, she asked, "I'll have lots of questions but first could we go outside so I can get your picture with the Gulf in the background?"

After Ben stood up, she continued, "Bring everything with you—including the spear."

Chuck stayed with the bar while Cal and Ben went outside. They walked to a strip of sand at the water's edge. People nearby stared at the strange, wild man walking with the woman who carried a camera. "Must be a reporter," said one man before he followed a woman into the bar.

While waves crashed along the shore and pelicans flew past skimming the surface, Cal took picture after picture of Ben with his deep tan, rough shorts, tools, and particularly, holding his spear.

"At least one of these pictures should make the front page," she said to Ben after concluding her work. "Chuck's bar and resort will likely get a lot busier when this story reaches the public."

Pointing to lounge chairs shaded by coconut palms, she continued, "Could we sit over there while I ask you some questions?"

"Of course," he answered. "I'll meet you there. First I must see Chuck."

"Okay," she replied before Ben searched under a few layers of material comprising his shorts. He withdrew a money belt then selected cash. After replacing the belt, he walked to the bar as Cal proceeded to the shaded chairs.

Inside the bar, Ben approached Chuck who was filling glasses with draft. Giving Chuck the cash, Ben said, "This will cover the meal and two extra tall cans of beer. Please make one of the cans something that Cal likes."

Accepting the money, Chuck put it in the till then gave Ben one can. Extending to him the second can, he said, "This is for Cal."

"Thank you," said Ben, receiving the beer.

"You're a man of surprises," noted Chuck. "You said you could pay and I always take a person by his or her word until I have a reason not to. Although that's true, I'm still surprised to see you with cash. Your story is going to increase business—likely greatly. I could use help with everything, particularly the resort. Work would entail the whole ball of wax from cleaning rooms, to repairs, and tending bar. Job is yours if you're interested."

"I could do that—while I sort my life out again and adjust to being away from the wilderness," Ben replied. "I'm from Ontario."

"I can look after government regulations," confirmed Chuck. "Anyone who can get thrown into a swamp and come out on top as you did has all the ability required to help run a resort with lots left over. You have demonstrated that you can work independently without requiring a lot of supervision."

"Good idea then," said Ben. "Thank you."

"You'll need to get some clothes of course," added Chuck. "I can supply room and as much board as you want—along with the use of resort vehicles and boats."

"Thank you again," said Ben before he took the two refreshments to the chairs where Calley waited.

Receiving the can, Cal said, "Thoughtful of you. My favorite."

"I have reliable references," responded Ben before sitting down. He looked across the sand to waves where a pelican dove for a fish. "Thanks for talking outside. I might never be comfortable again inside buildings."

He removed the copper pot, pottery cup, rusted knife, and an ax. Lastly, he added a copper container with line and hooks. "These are all the items I took from the settlers' cabin site. The head of this ax is from there and of course the knife, pot, and cup. Giving them to her, he continued, "These objects are for you. I appreciate having temporary use of them. To keep everything together, you can also keep the other things I have made such as knives, an ax, and a spear."

"Thoughtful of you again," she declared. "I'll treasure these."

"By the way, you are now talking to an employee of the *End of the Road Beach Resort*," he said. "I just got hired to help look after the place—cleaning rooms, repairs, and bar."

"That's good news," she exclaimed. "Chuck is smart. He knows your story will draw customers and he's going to get much busier. You've also proven yourself to have many good qualities or you would not have survived. I should warn you that any information you tell me could end up in your story—and the reporting started as soon as I heard about you."

"Okay," he said before taking a long sip of the cold drink. "Getting good drinking water was a constant concern. The copper pot really helped."

"How did all this start?" she asked, becoming more noticeably a reporter.

"In the office at work in Ontario," he started, "the atmosphere there and my life had faded to a shade of gray. So I went on a holiday and flew south to Florida, rented a car then started driving to a resort.

A tire blew and I was stranded at the roadside. I just finished the repairs when two guys in a truck stopped. They both aimed guns at me and stole my most accessible cash along with the car—and luggage. I heard them arguing about having to kill me so I ran into an adjacent border of foliage. When a shot zipped past my head, I moved as fast as possible with them in pursuit. I lost them but I got lost too. You can't cry about what you haven't got. You have to work with what you do have. I made a life in the wild—to such an extent I entered it fully, no longer considering it wild or strange but I came to have this perspective only about the outside world—the one I had left behind. In what I thought at the beginning was wild I found life and my life. I'll never be the same again. I came to realize the surrounding foliage, trees, landscape, wildlife, and myself were all connected—particularly spiritually and everything in its own way was in balance—in a world of hard knocks all with the purpose of molding each one, all spirits to their finest potential. The center of it all and connecting to each other part is an always-kind

Creator. If a spirit moves toward the Creator, there is life. In moving away a spirit self-makes the only hell there is. I am at home now in the natural world and will never be at rest again in a town or city."

"How did you get all these ideas?" she asked.

"I had heard different possibilities before getting lost in the forest," he explained. "Out there, alone, I became faced with the truth contained in previous information and saw life, my life, for the first time, realizing out in the swamp I was not alone but in company with truth I had previously not believed. I came to see, actually believe and feel at home. Some people might call my experience a journey of insightful realization."

"I like the depth of your journey," stated Cal. She looked directly at him and her eyes were very light brown. "You lived—maybe for the first time. You didn't just survive you found life. You found you."

"Maybe I found some of you too," he added. "I seem to have located the cabin of your ancestry."

"I would like you to take me to this cabin site as soon as you are free to do so," she requested.

"As soon as possible," he agreed. "Might be difficult to find the location. Not impossible though. I built an elaborate shelter between the cabin site and the Gulf.

A policewoman walked down from the bar. She approached Ben and Calley. The officer was a heavy-set, robust person with blonde hair protruding below her hat. Her eyes were light blue. Standing in front of Ben, she adjusted her gun belt and declared, "My detective training tells me you're the suspect."

"What gave me away?" he asked.

"On—a number of things," she pondered. "But you know I think maybe—it was the spear."

Turning to look at both Ben and Cal, she continued, "I'm Sal—actually Sally."

Pointing to Calley, Ben explained, "Cal—the best reporter with long-time connections to this area. I'm Ben—the long-missing Benteen Sands."

"I took this call," said Sal. "I wasn't going to hand it off to anyone else. When you're ready, I'd like to take you to the office. We've all had work in your case and we have lots of questions."

"I'm sure Chuck would have some clothes I could wear—maybe a shave and haircut," he offered.

"Don't spoil a thing," she declared. "Just as you are. When you're ready I'll be up by the cruiser."

"Okay," he said. "Do I bring the spear?"

"Spear too," she shouted. "Just as you are."

"You're going to be busy for a while," said Cal. "When you come back and start working for Chuck, I'd appreciate a visit to that homestead."

"When you're ready, I'm ready," he assured her. "We could go when I get back from the police station."

"Okay," she said. They both stood up and started walking to the parking lot. "Thanks for the story."

"Don't forget to say that the guy was great looking," he added.

"The person I've met is great, but I'm not sure I've actually seen him," she replied, smiling then turned toward her car.

Ben repeated his story to Sally on the way to the station where he was a hit—a sensation. Most people there had in one way or another been involved with his case. Next to a side road, his rental car had been found undamaged and just out of gas. The police contacted the rental company and Ben also talked to them. He had use of the station for a shower then he cut off the longest parts of both hair and beard. He was also given some extra clothes to assist him with his next stop and that was to buy clothes. Lastly, he entered a hair salon.

"Shave and a haircut two bits—as the saying goes," he said as he approached the waiting stylist.

"Yes," she answered, "plus a lot more."

"Inflation has hit everything," he noted before sitting down in her chair.

"Yes, it has," she agreed.

"Could I get a shave please and hair tidied up?" he asked.

"This makes my day," she exclaimed before starting. "I like a challenge. Why did you decide to change your look?"

"I came back to town," he replied.

"Maybe I'm asking too many questions," she continued, "but where did you go?"

"I came to Florida for a vacation and got robbed," he explained. "Before the bandits could shoot me I ran into a wilderness. Although I got lost in a place I at first saw as being hostile I later enjoyed living there. I just came back and reported to the police today."

Stepping back, she exclaimed, "You're that guy—the wild guy who was thought to be dead but came back."

"The same one," he confirmed.

"You're Ben Sands," she declared.

"Right again," he said.

"Well," she exclaimed before returning to her efforts. "This is the first time I've worked on a dead guy."

"This is the first time I've been a dead guy," he added.

"Welcome back," she declared. "You must be relieved your ordeal is over."

"It was an ordeal at first—then I started to enjoy the wilderness," he explained. "In my quiet times now I find myself missing the wild. I plan to go back whenever I can."

"Like the old story of throwing a rabbit into a brier patch," she suggested.

"Beauty may be really in the eye of the beholder," he observed.

After concentrating quietly on her efforts, she said, "You're finished. You might not recognize yourself."

They both walked to the front counter where Ben paid his bill, adding a good tip.

"Been a pleasure," she concluded.

Turning to leave, he said, "I hope you lied and made me look great."

"I didn't—and you do," she countered, laughing.

"Thanks," he added before leaving the building. He rented a room at a motel for a few nights to adjust to being back while he also shopped for food and general supplies. With preparations having been made, he returned to the police station where he asked for and received a ride to the resort.

He entered the bar and approached Chuck who had just brought a glass of draft to a customer. Seeing Ben, Chuck asked, "What will you be having?"

"A job maybe," he answered. "I think possibly I work here."

Staring while stroking his beard, Chuck whispered, "I would never have picked you out in a lineup. Can't be—but you are. Strange it is how I'd hire a guy without even seeing him. How many people are you?"

"Maybe two," answered Ben, enjoying the reaction—"one before and one now—in appearance."

"Well you can both start right away," declared Chuck. "Calley's story about you has already increased business. I'm going to have to hire another bartender. Rooms are renting too. I hired you because your survival—even prospering—in the wild shows you can work on your own without supervision. You don't need to have someone telling you what to do all the time. You're a self-starter and independent."

Walking with Ben toward the door, Chuck asked, "Could you start right away?"

"Yes," he replied before they stepped outside into the sunlight where a greater number of people were on the beach.

"I'll show you around," Chuck directed. Leading a tour, he explained, "You can work at anything anywhere on the resort, including the bar. Your main job however will be in charge of rooms. I'll look after bookings at the office until you get accustomed to our procedures. Right now you can center on maintenance and cleaning rooms along with looking after customer requests. The back place will be your living quarters. That's room one. There's a bed, kitchen, general space, and washroom. The resort jeep is yours to use. Rooms must be clean—bedding washed after each customer leaves. Keep places stocked with items to get customers started. You can be in charge of your work schedule. That's a quality in particular that I like in you. Any questions?"

"There's a topic I'd like to add," replied Ben. "At dawn and dusk, I'd like to take a chair, cast net, pail, and fishing pole to the water's edge and do some fishing. I would cook some fish for meals in the room. Other fillets I could take to the restaurant and then add Catch of the Day as an item on the menu. Customers would also fish and I could help them. They could have their catches cooked for them at the restaurant."

"Good idea," declared Chuck. "I'm all for it. Since you've been here, there have been more fishermen at the beach."

"If available, a present tool shed or a new structure could be established as a fish-cleaning house," suggested Ben.

"You can set one up in the unused shed at the back," noted Chuck. "There's a sink in there along with a table." Straightening up and looking around, he declared, "The earth has shifted and we're in a better place."

"We certainly are," agreed Ben. "This job has been designed for me."

"You're the right person in the right place at the right time," observed Chuck.

"Thanks to you," added Ben.

"And you," countered Chuck. Giving Ben a check, he explained, "This is your first month's pay. It will get you started. Raises will follow in the future. Extending another payment, he said, "This second check can be used to pay for meals and drinks at the bar. Two payments will come each month. You might want to get started by taking the jeep to get groceries, fishing equipment, and other stuff. Work will begin when you're ready."

Receiving the checks, Ben said, "Thanks for taking a chance on me."

"I don't take chances," Chuck stated. "Welcome to the *End of the Road Beach Resort*. Because of additional customers, you're already attracting, I have to hire another bartender. Of course, you're also one."

Chuck returned to the bar. Ben used the jeep to drive to the bank and cash the checks. Afterward, he stocked up on groceries and fishing equipment along with extra clothes and other supplies.

The next days found him at home in his room at the back corner of the resort. The buildings were constructed with a main restaurant and bar area adjacent to a general office followed by Ben's room with rental rooms extending farther out toward the beach. Behind the rental rooms, there was one of three parking lots. Others were at the front of both the office and bar.

The work suited Ben perfectly. He enjoyed doing repairs. Knowing the vital importance of cleanliness in any business especially one involving food and lodging, he enthusiastically met the challenge of keeping rooms clean. He cooked some meals at his own residence along with sometimes dining at the bar and occasionally visiting nearby restaurants. Dust and dawn usually found him fishing at the water's edge. He took the catch of the day to the bar's restaurant while he also cooked some of the catch in his room.

Sometimes work is perfectly suited to a person, he observed in his room after he sat down in a favorite chair, put his leg up on a table in front then sipped beer from a glass. In front, there was a television backed by a window providing a view outside to palms bordering a walkway beside the rental rooms. With the day's work finished, evening fishing completed and last meal cooked, I enjoy this interval to relax and consider the day past in addition to the new one to begin.

One morning, the rising sun, as usual, found Ben leaving the beach and returning to his room after some dawn fishing. He approached Calley who had left her car and was walking toward the bar's restaurant. When she walked past Ben, he stared at her, smiling. Both intrigued and annoyed, she turned to him and asked, "You always stare at people?"

"I do when people I know walk past and don't speak," he answered, smiling again.

"Oh," she exclaimed, looking at him more carefully. "I know the person—and the eyes," she whispered, "but I can't place where I've—"

Her face brightened before she asked, "You're not?"

"Yes," he stated. "We're both here. The one you see and the wild guy."

Laughing, she exclaimed, "You clean up well. The eyes I remembered. Ready to go to the homestead?"

"Any time you want to go," he replied.

"My boyfriend said he'd take us in his boat," she explained. "I'll call him."

"I'll be ready and I'll tell Chuck I'll be away," he confirmed.

"Thanks," she said before continuing to walk toward the bar's entrance.

Calling to her, Ben added, "He showed me your wonderful stories. A great looking guy on the front covers."

"Oh," she said. "You're the first one who thought so."

"I have to take my catch of the day to the cook," continued Ben.

"The catch of my lifetime is going to be that homestead," declared Calley. "See you soon." She proceeded to the front door while Ben had fish to look after.

Meeting again at the water's edge, Calley said, "Chuck told me your presence here—and my stories—have greatly increased customers. With your help, they've been fishing and having their catches cooked at the bar's restaurant. Resort rooms are almost always fully occupied. You're looking after the place well and keeping rooms so clean people have been mentioning it. Your presence here has been the best thing that has happened to the *End of the Road Beach Resort*."

"That's all good news—like your stories," responded Ben.

The boat was approaching and with its appearance, Ben had his first warning. The craft was built to impress with style and speed rather than for practicality and seaworthiness. "Is your friend like his boat?" asked Ben.

"You're not impressed by his boat are you?" she asked.

"No," he stated.

"I'm not either," she confided. "It's only good because I don't have one."

When the craft nudged the shore Cal and Ben scrambled onto a long, sleek bow. Aboard, Cal introduced the two men and Ben shook hands with a person who seemed to be an extension of the boat. Carey Stiller had light brown hair swept back into a bun. His eyes were pale blue and avoided looking directly at another's glance. He seemed to be of moderate height, weight, and strength although an apparent assertiveness indicated he tried to push beyond abilities, always trying to impress.

"Follow the shore westward for a while then we should move slowly and as close to shore as possible," offered Ben to both Carey and Calley.

The boat reversed and turned before leveling off at amazing speed, heading westward during an average day with a slight breeze and moderate waves under an almost endlessly blue sky. Only a few clouds drifted along with a frigate bird.

After waiting for a seemingly appropriate time, Ben pointed toward the shore. With reduced speed, the craft turned shoreward bringing closer its rugged terrain. "We should closely check the sandy coves," suggested Ben. "I built a shelter on one of them and that's the landmark we want to find."

While the morning drifted past with tranquility as the feature of the day, a search continued beside a seemingly impenetrable shoreline that was almost without visible land. Finally Ben said, "We must've gone past it. We should go back and try to find a sandy cove. Maybe there are very few places where a boat can come right to shore."

The search took longer than Carey's interest lasted. Objects brushing against the boat turned annoyance into anger when he declared, "We're not going to find anything." More directly to Calley, he said, "You've been years searching with little results. Today's going to be no different. A search like this needs a smaller boat. This craft is built for speed, not mangrove swamps."

"If we can actually land on sand in a cove, we will be in one of very few such places and likely the right one," offered Ben. To break the growing tension, he asked, "How did you two meet?"

"I work in a gym," stated Carey. "I'm a personal trainer. Calley used to come in and exercise."

"Not anymore," she added. "Now I like to swim in the Gulf and walk for miles along the beach."

"Good ideas," exclaimed Ben. "We should get exercise naturally. If that's not happening, we should change our lifestyles."

"That would put me out of business," stated Carey. "Most people are out o' shape and should go to a gym—and get help too." With frustration and anger adding sharpness to his voice, he said, "This search isn't working."

"Land at the next cove," directed Calley.

Leaving the one they were in, Carey increased speed and entered another. Fortunately, with little risk to the craft, the bow touched the shore.

They jumped out and in a short time, Ben said, "Not the place. We should try farther east."

In the boat again, Carey passed around cans of beer then the journey continued until another break appeared in a mainly impenetrable shoreline. "I'll never quit," declared Calley.

"I quit a long time ago," admitted Carey.

"Thanks for tolerating this quest," said Calley. "Just consider it exercise at the gym and we're pushing ourselves to the limit."

He glared at her but quickly had to turn his attention to one obstacle after another.

"In this type of landscape I lived for a long time," explained Ben. "After you've been here long enough you become able to see beauty. It's here just the way it should be. Some people are the same—only inhospitable on the outside."

"Some people are nuts too," stated Carey. "I'll be relieved when Cal calls this thing off."

When the bow brushed up against sand, the three people scrambled onto the shore. Cal and Carey secured the boat while Ben quickly moved out of view beyond a barrier of foliage. "I'm home!" he shouted. "This is the place!"

"You found your shelter?" asked Cal.

"It's here," he called back.

"After all these years," she gasped as she picked a route through the foliage. Carey followed her.

She stood in wonder while all three people looked at a structure held off the ground by palm logs. On this base, a cabin stood made of the same logs in addition to mangrove poles and vines. Palmetto leaves topped the roof. A ladder led to the interior.

"I have to say," observed Carey, speaking mainly to Ben. "I suppose it's obvious I'm not interested in this trip. You and I don't and likely won't get along—but that is an impressive building. I'm going up to look inside."

"I will later," said Calley. "First though Ben, I want to see the homestead."

Starting to walk farther inland, Ben replied, "Back here."

Calley followed and soon shouted, "Orange trees!"

"Delicious oranges too," added Ben.

"This is the site," stated Cal, standing beside the outline marked in the ground. "For years I've searched," she whispered. "Thanks to you, Ben, I've found it. This is the place my ancestors, Charles and Winnifred, came about 1850. They lived the rest of their lives at this site. They planted orange trees."

Opening her pack, she said, "I have a camera. I'll take pictures and write new stories. The first accounts about you were successes. A continuing series will be welcomed."

"As I mentioned earlier," said Ben, "the things I found here are yours—including the spear and you might find other items."

"You sure about the spear?" she asked while using a stick to poke around the edges of the homestead outlined in the soil.

"Yes," he replied. "All mementos should be in one place."

Walking to the site, Carey said, "That's quite a building Ben."

"I'll take pictures of your shelter later," noted Calley. "Going to make wonderful stories."

"Wow!" she shouted. "I've dislodged something of rusted metal with a chain on it." Rubbing the item, cleaning it, she exclaimed, "A locket."

"You'll need this," said Carey, giving her a knife. She used its blade to pry between edges and the object opened into two halves hinged together. On each side, there was a portrait. One was a man and the other a woman.

"This is priceless," she whispered. "They would be my great grandparents. When I think of all the years I've searched—and now I've found them."

"You could come back with a metal detector," suggested Carey.

"Yes," she agreed. "I will."

Further searching located a broken pottery bowl along with a cup. Satisfied with her discoveries for one day, she joined the others in enjoying oranges.

"I'd like to have a look inside your shelter," said Calley to Ben, "and get more pictures. There are a bunch of stories here. The *End of the Road Beach Resort* will get more customers than can be accommodated. Chuck told me this morning he just hired another bartender—one of the customers, called George Wiggins. His dad ran a fruit stand where he sold oranges and grapefruit he picked from his own trees."

"Come and see this cabin," offered Carey, leading the way. "No wonder Ben enjoyed staying here. You both get started. I'll be back."

After they climbed the ladder, Ben sat on the floor and leaned his back against a wall, leaving the two chairs for Cal and Carey. "Thanks, Ben," said Cal after sitting down. Your shelter is incredible. You really made a home here. You must've been sorry to leave."

"I would've been sorry if I had left," he answered as her eyes widened in astonishment. "I did not leave the wild," he continued. "It came with me, lives with me in my awareness. I can go back in memory or look around at any natural environment and see the garden of the Creator where everything is connected and we are part of the others—spiritually."

Writing in her notebook, Calley exclaimed, "Wow. I would like to live here someday and search for what you have found. Also, in this place, I can connect with the lives of my ancestors for whom I have searched for so long."

"I understand what you are saying," responded Ben as Calley kept writing. "There is no such thing as one spirit alone. All are connected—even the present with the past. Everything is one story. Your ancestors provide many good examples for today because they did not wreck the environment, leaving destruction for the future as many industries are doing today. Spiritual life is the only important life and all that lasts forever. So why seek the temporary?"

"As you see," said Calley, "I'm making notes. I'm almost always writing. Can I add your views of what you found here to my next accounts?"

"Of course," he answered. "Words also make a thousand pictures."

"Your time of getting lost in the swamp could've been so much worse than it became for you," she said, almost whispering. "Much of life is planned and I seek that plan—to stay on track. But we also have choices. Rather than being destroyed, you found more here than what you had left behind. Maybe all obstacles are opportunities. What a wonderful view of life. Right now I'm going to start writing a memoir of my life and title it *Lost No Longer*. That's true for you and me too. Thanks to you I found the homestead of my family that I came south to discover—and you located it for me. Here I have connected with my own past and likely my future. You have experienced the same journey of life. What a story I'm catching."

Carey climbed the ladder. He brought a six-pack of beer and distributed drinks before sitting down on the remaining chair. "Ben, your cabin is well constructed," he exclaimed with an obvious appreciation of the structure. "I see Cal has started her next articles. She'll have lots of pictures to go with them."

"Thanks for bringing the treats," said Cal. "We're celebrating what Ben found here—what I've found—and with my descriptions, many will discover. The only part I'll leave out will be the exact location of this site. I don't want this shelter or homestead overrun with visitors."

"Ben is a story and Calley writes the story," observed Carey.

"Thanks for thinking of the beer," said Ben.

"Thought it fit the occasion," replied Carey. "Do you do a lot of building?"

"I like making things," answered Ben. "During this so-called vacation, I've learned to connect with the wilderness. I've also enjoyed being part of the *End of the Road Beach Resort*. When I return to the north, I'll maybe combine both parts of this trip and build a lodge in the wilderness."

"When you get cabins ready to rent, send us your address," said Carey.

"Okay," agreed Ben. "The lodge here is a success. Customers are lining up."

"Thanks to your adventure that Calley has been describing," observed Carey.

Putting away her notes, she said, "I have more wonderful events to report. This is a special place—and I've searched for it all my life. Each person should watch for the special places—those that touch an individual—along with other locations that can be experienced by many people. I've heard of thin places where the spiritual dimension shines through or at least is more noticeable. This is such a spot for me—as it has been for Ben. I like Ben's statement that he did not leave because this experience—the wild—stayed with him. I feel that way when I write these articles. They just didn't happen—they live."

Carey distributed the second round of drinks while each visitor enjoyed the wilderness. After they left the shelter and started walking to the boat, Cal said, "Maybe we didn't just find a shelter or a homestead. We have seen a landmark, a buoy, showing us we are on the right course during our journeys. There are such occasions when I feel I'm where I should be at this time doing what I am supposed to be doing. Sometimes everything seems wrong; yet there are other times, like now, when all things seem right, just as they are meant to be."

"Sure feels that way," noted Ben.

"And I have more adventures to write about," added Calley.

During the ride back in the boat, each person considered immediate plans. Calley had more to add to the series of articles she had been writing about Ben and his adventures. Now she could mention how his journey had located her ancestors' early home. Carey would go back to his work at the gym. Ben knew he would be busy helping to accommodate all the customers attracted by Calley's articles.

Dolphins jumped in the wake formed by the speeding boat. They seemed to feel the same sense of celebration enjoyed by the three people. When Ben was left at the resort, Calley said, "I'll bring you copies of our story."

The words, "our story," Ben repeated over and over to himself during his work. He seemed always to be busy. Cleaning rooms after the departure of each customer was a priority. His favorite efforts occurred when he helped people learn not just to fish but the art of fishing. There were numerous beginners who had to be helped not only with equipment but also filleting. Many people wanted their catch of the day cooked for meals at the restaurant. Ben usually cooked in his room. Following each meal, he looked forward to quiet times when the day's work was finished and he had a chance to rest in the room or outside. Sometimes he would sit on a sandbank bordering the beach. Here he would reflect on the previous day along with others both of the past or future.

When Calley brought him copies of her most recent accounts involving the shelter along with her ancestor's homestead, he invited her to a restaurant he had discovered a few miles away beside the Gulf Intracoastal Waterway.

They arrived early. Ben parked on a lot facing the water. Commercial fishing and tour boats were tied at docks in front of the restaurant. The water was calm. Occasionally a fish stirred the surface sending ripples toward banks of mangroves. Pelicans flew leisurely across the sky.

When a woman unlocked the main door to the restaurant, Calley led the way, entered the building, and selected a table next to open windows facing the water. To their table walked a woman who displayed calm assurance in her attitude honed through years of experience that also left behind a few lines. Grayish-black hair bordered her face where brown eyes sparkled when she said, "Our first customers, starting a new day. Anything from the bar?"

"I was going to have a draft," answered Cal, "but I have draft days and Margarita days. This seems more like a time for a Margarita."

"Celebrating?" asked the woman.

"Yes," replied Cal. "Many good things have been happening recently."

Turning to look at Ben, the woman asked, "And what would one of the good things have?"

"Not sure that I qualify," he answered, getting the women laughing. "I only have draft days."

"The woman said, "I'm Lilly.""

Pointing to Calley, Ben said, "Cal—and I'm Ben."

The drinks arrived quickly and were sipped slowly while Ben and Cal relaxed, enjoying the welcoming atmosphere of the restaurant as it gathered to itself all features of a summer day of rest beside the Gulf.

"You said your great grandparents were Winnifred McCord originally from Scotland and Charles Nelson who was English," recalled Ben.

"Yes," replied Calley who enjoyed his interest in a past she had tried to locate most of her adult life. "Their son and daughter moved to the Canadian side of the prairie and settled near Claresholm, Alberta. They swam in Willow Creek. Also, they fished in the Little Bow River, Old Man River, and Trout Creek. When these two settlers got established in a homestead they met people whom they married then moved east. I'm from Ontario and have always searched for the Florida homestead that you found."

"Have you been to the Claresholm homestead?" he asked.

"Yes," she replied.

"You seem very interested in the past," observed Ben.

"Yes," she stated, "because there's no such thing as past. I'm a reporter and have learned there are no such things as past, present or future. There is only one story that is all connected, particularly spiritually. We ignore one of these aspects at our own peril. Those who have lived here before us have much to instruct the present population as we all guide the future. Everything is connected to each other with all aspects having part of a common spark of the Creator."

"You learned that information by being a reporter of life and I heard the same message by getting lost in the swamp," added Ben. "I remained lost until I realized I was actually home. I was in the place I was seeking by going on a vacation. Were the two guys who tried to kill me really criminals or were they just helping me to get home?"

"We might ask," said Cal, "if everything is planned out for us why should we bother doing anything? Of course only the spiritual outline is established. We have the freedom to make and are responsible for choices we select along the way. They determine our development in striving for our finest identity. We learn by choosing. The choices of unique individuals make each life's experience different and new. They all make parts of one story. That's what I do. I'm a story reporter."

"The best of them too," added Ben.

"If you had made different decisions in the swamp, the outcome could've been disastrous," observed Calley. "That's why Chuck hired you. You withdrew success out of potential defeat."

"I wasn't planning to do this but I think I'll have another draft," said Ben.

"Okay," agreed Cal. "You just talked me into having another Margarita." She pointed to the drinks and Lilly brought two more.

When they arrived, Ben explained to Lilly, "We're celebrating. Even the cook seems to be in a good mood. Have you noticed he keeps singing about Portobello?"

"That's our special," said Lilly. "It's portobello mushroom stuffed with crab meat topped by Swiss cheese and tomato then served with a salad."

"You talked me into having that for lunch," said Cal.

"And for you?" Lilly asked Ben.

"Grouper sandwich please—with cheese," he replied.

"What kind o' crab meat is on the mushroom?" asked Cal.

"Blue crab," answered Lilly.

"Is that what fishermen in boats are emptying from traps along the shore here?" enquired Cal.

"Yes," she replied before leaving to place the orders.

"I'm going to do a story on this restaurant," said Calley.

"Good idea," noted Ben. "Your articles have brought a rush of business to the *End of the Road Beach Resort*. We are always booked. The restaurant's bar is full."

"Your information did that," noted Cal.

"I like your reports," stated Ben. "Pictures are great too."

"As we were saying," continued Cal, "the past is the present. We ignore the past at our peril. My great grandparents' homestead was difficult to find and likely would not have been discovered if you had not sort of stumbled upon it. That's the impact those settlers had on the environment, leaving it mainly as they found it. Of course some individuals, such as those who slaughtered the buffalo, wrecked the environment. Today we have ignored good examples of the past and many people think an acceptable—even inevitable or necessary—part of business practices includes the destruction of land, water, or air to get resources such as logs, oil, gas, or minerals. The tar sands in northern

Alberta are leaving poisons and scars that may never cure. Today people's actions are so destructive they are wrecking even the weather."

When the meals arrived, Cal after doing some sampling said, "The cook was right to sing about the Portobello."

"You made a good choice," noted Ben. "I almost always request a grouper sandwich with cheese—except in Hawaii. There the best catch is mahi mahi or tuna."

During the meal, Ben took time to notice or just suddenly realized he was in one of those moments, the perfect snapshots of life that in itself was the way it should be to an almost magical or definitely spiritual extent and should be savored as such perfection in this way might never appear again. Cal's company was special as was the setting with open windows bringing in scents of the Gulf to fill the room and sprinkle it with a special joy of life. A spell was cast adding a glow to the moment— and its memory.

Noticing Ben staring out the window, Cal asked, "Nice trip?"

"Yes," he answered. "The journey wasn't away though. I was enjoying being right here."

"So am I," she added. "This is one of those occasions when all aspects combine in perfection that is momentarily glimpsed then is gone but the feeling such moments leave behind is never forgotten. Maybe at such times the other side, or spiritual world, joins with this one and we glimpse life when we are home."

After the visit to the restaurant, Ben and Calley returned to work where Cal wrote about legends and Ben had become one. The resort became almost too busy, continuing each day at full capacity. Requirements of customers took much and often all of Ben's time.

Occasionally he rushed a day's tasks in order to do some fishing before sunset. During one of these restful evenings, Cal met him at the water's edge. She brought a chair and sat down before giving Ben one of two cans of beer she carried.

"Thank you," he said, receiving the drink. "You are the catch of the day."

"So now I'm a fish," she exclaimed, laughing. "And there are a lot of fish in the sea."

"I'm beginning to think there's only one," he replied. "Only one visits me on the beach. Could I take you to another restaurant?"

"Is it as good as the last one?" she asked.

"You can tell me after you have been there," he answered.

"What time?" she asked.

"As soon as the food arrives," he said. When the pole bounced and the reel screamed, he added, "Maybe dinner has arrived. Would you like to bring it in?"

Cal smiled and Ben gave her the pole. The battle was sharp but short, ending with a large, king mackerel coming to shore.

Cal helped carry the fish along with equipment to Ben's room where she looked after other projects while Ben did the filleting. Before the fillets had cooked to the preferred golden color, he walked to the bar and returned carrying two Margaritas.

When other preparations had been completed, the drinks were tried first. Putting down her glass beside the prepared meal in the small room, Calley looked at Ben and said, "Took a lot of work to get ready for this meal in contrast to the other but our efforts increase our appreciation of what we have."

"As we stopped to sip Margaritas I got a glimpse of how lucky I am to have you here," observed Ben.

"The other restaurant added entertainment to life," she noted. "This meal is life."

"I've started to see you that way," he added.

Without more words, the meal continued. After a short time, he said, "Where fish is concerned, how good it is depends on how fresh it is."

"That explains why this meal is such a pleasure," added Cal. "Maybe we could go to the beach, wait an appropriate time then go for a swim?"

"Good idea," he noted. "Maybe you could walk to the beach with towels and I'll meet you there."

"Okay," she answered.

She proceeded to the beach. Ben met her soon afterward and gave her one of two Margaritas he carried.

"You saved me a trip," she said, smiling after receiving the drink.

Looking around at the sand, water, and sky, Ben observed, "People can't make anything like this. Amazing though how people respect their buildings and take natural beauty for granted as if it is so endless we can wreck it without consequences. If people realized natural beauty is limited they would respect and cherish it."

"As you said before, it is part of us," reflected Calley.

"That's what I learned when I ran into the wilderness to escape from two bandits who were going to kill me," continued Ben. "In a way, they did kill me. They killed the way I was before. In the wilderness I found life. I realized I was in the Creator's garden. The spirit of the garden is also in us, as with each living thing. Maintaining this connection keeps us on the right course while we face obstacles and thereby keep learning, always seeking improvements. By seeing and recognizing the natural world, I found myself. I did not leave the wild because I brought it with me when I walked to the **End of the Road Beach Resort**."

"Again," exclaimed Calley, "you have given me another story. This calls for another Margarita." Standing, she added, "I'll be right back."

The restaurant's bar supplied Margaritas as the landscape set a panorama of changing and moving harmony. A light, salty breeze sent waves splashing along the shore, and rattling palm leaves added a background song to more distinct calls of gulls while the setting sun withdrew vibrant scarlet hues from approaching night. Into this changing realm, the moon brought increasing light, brightening cresting waves breaking along the sand. Calley and Ben did not realize the night had slipped past until sunlight flashed upon the water and land.

Cal left and started a series of new articles explaining what Ben had learned while living in the wild. Ben resumed work, becoming almost constantly busy.

As usual, at the end of each day, he tried to find time to go fishing. When fish did not bite, there was always something else happening such as constantly changing patterns of clouds or actions of birds in a natural world where sameness includes constant movement. Days moved past, becoming lost in a routine of constant requests from tourists.

When work was completed, Ben continued the habit of relaxing in a chair outside his room. Palms provided shade while the vastness of the Gulf almost always sent a breeze to refresh the land.

Routines broke one day when evening shadows found Ben relaxing in one of the chairs outside his room. Chuck Canby arrived, carrying two draft glasses and a pitcher of beer. He sat down on a chair next to

Ben. After filling a glass for Ben then one for himself, Chuck placed the pitcher on the arm of a third chair.

Both men savored a long sample of a draft before Chuck said, "I came to apologize. I should've told you sooner or discussed this with you but an event caught us both by surprise. I was offered so much money for my resort I could only accept."

Alarm shot through Ben. He realized that the world for him had just shifted.

"Anyone can see that you brought this about," continued Chuck. "Before you arrived, I could hardly stay in business—and accordingly, there were no offers to purchase. Your sensational arrival attracted so much attention we are now fully booked all the time. This place is booming. People with a lot of money are going to expand the resort in all ways with more and larger of everything such as elaborate rental units, a grander restaurant, and bar, along with docks, boats—the works. I had the buyer cut two large checks—one for me and one for you."

Receiving the envelope, Ben looked inside and could not believe the fortune he had just obtained. "Very, very generous of you," he exclaimed. "Many people—maybe most—would not have included me."

"You made this happen," explained Chuck. "You have received one-third of the payment and I two-thirds because I have supplied the resort. You made it successful."

"I'm shocked—happily—to receive this portion yet sorry your resort has gone," reflected Ben. "What are you going to do?"

"Invest the money and retire," he answered. "Now I'll have time to do some of the things I've missed. What will you do?"

"I came here on a vacation—some vacation," he replied. "Since my job is finished I'll go back north. I'll have to tell Calley. Does she know about this?"

"You and I are the first to know—and of course my wife and daughter," he said. "Haven't heard from Calley since she told me she was getting married—to Carey Stiller."

This news struck Ben. He tried to hide the impact. Noticing how his friend struggled with the information, Chuck said, "I thought you would know."

"I didn't know," countered Ben. "When will the job here end?"

"We aren't taking any new bookings," he explained. "We'll follow through with those we have then the place will close. You and I can stay until that time—one month from now—or, if we want to, we can leave earlier and the new owners will use other people to finish."

"Since the resort has gone—along with you and Calley—I'll make arrangements now to go north," noted Ben. "I have you to thank—along with Calley—for the time of my life more wonderful than words I can express to sufficiently thank you."

"We are each part of this," observed Chuck.

"Along with everything else, your draft beer is appreciated," said Ben.

"I thought it would help with the news I was bringing," confessed Chuck.

"You have always been considerate," noted Ben.

After collecting the empty glasses along with the pitcher, Chuck stood up and said, "We both have plans to make."

"Thank you for including me in the payment," added Ben.

"You earned it," concluded Chuck before he walked away, moving out of view amid shadows.

Ben could not move. He slept little that night and packed in the morning. The next day, he looked through the plane's window and watched as the Gulf and its shoreline brightened at sunset then gradually became obscured by clouds.

CHAPTER TWO

NORTHLAND

When Ben returned to Ontario, he discovered, as he had expected, that he had been replaced at his previous place of employment. Next, he also sold his condo. After packing his car with the remnant of his possessions in addition to supplies for a trip of unknown length, he rented a cabin for one night.

The structure was one of several cabins built on a rock outcropping extending into a sandy inlet of Georgian Bay. Sitting inside, beside a propane fueled fireplace, he looked out through windows providing a panoramic view of rocky islands set in a blue, shimmering vastness of water.

Once again, he reflected, I've been thrown into a swamp—a wilderness. This time, however, the situation is different because I'm no longer lost in this wilderness or any other. I'm at home. All I have to do now is build a physical structure of a home. It will resemble the *End of the Road Beach Resort* while also incorporating some of the features of this cabin resort where I'm now staying. These buildings adapt to this particular wilderness. First I must look for a piece of land—in the wilderness—where I'll build my lodge.

The next morning, after breakfast, he packed the car. Before leaving, he sat down to enjoy a cup of coffee and watch the first rays of sunlight flash across the islands of Georgian Bay. When I was in Florida, he recalled, I found the homestead where Calley's great grandparents, Charles and Winnifred Nelson, settled approximately in 1850. They remained at this location all their lives. Their son and daughter moved north and settled near Claresholm, Alberta. Members of the family eventually moved eastward. Calley Nelson was from Ontario.

Carrying a cup of coffee to start the journey, Ben left the cabin, stepping into a refreshing breeze stirring inland from Georgian Bay. A heron stalked shallows near shore. Geese called while swimming in an adjacent reedy area.

As he drove away from the buildings, he felt the excitement of beginning a great adventure. Rarely does a person have the freedom in life to turn north, south, east, or west, he reflected. I have that liberty now. I've chosen a western journey, not out of necessity, as most directions are selected, but with total freedom that assures me that I'm on the right course. Calley traveled southward, wanting to locate the pioneering home established by her family. In finding this site, I have become part of the Nelson story. I know life is not haphazard and there's no such thing as coincidence. Everything is not set out because we have to make choices. However, parts are already established through sacred synchronism. The Nelson story has become part of my life. I'll complete this segment by finding or at least looking for the prairie homestead. The land I'm now driving across is the wilderness area where I'll build my resort that I'll call, *End of the Trail Cabins*. In Florida, I learned to be at home in the wilderness. I'll return to this northern, Georgian Bay area and build the physical structures of a home.

Even without a map, reasoned Ben, I could follow the progress of my journey by observing water and trees. Western mountains block much rainfall, leaving lush growth on the Pacific side and dry foothills to the east. Only farther eastward does moisture start returning to prevailing winds coming from the west. While I drive toward the prairie, the forests become less numerous, dwindling to pockets of aspens, willows, and predominantly cottonwoods. Lakes also diminish while sloughs become numerous along with eastward flowing rivers.

Rolling hills of the prairie are endlessly interesting, observed Ben because there is a panoramic view of vast distance circled by a horizon under a vast sky. Tragically almost every effort has been made to poison or shoot gophers that not only have their own lives to live but also provide a food base for numerous animals and birds.

I have enjoyed the first days of this journey, he reflected, and now I'm approaching Claresholm. In the town, he parked his car and walked to a center where older residents might gather. After entering the building, he realized instantly he was an outsider. The other occupants of the room stopped talking, looked at him while one lady asked, "What do you want?"

"I was looking for the homestead first settled by the Nelson family," he explained.

As other occupants started looking for records, one fellow stood up. He was tall and lanky, topped by white hair above a leathery face where blue eyes sparkled. He wore faded jeans kept in place by a wide belt centered with a silver buckle depicting a rider on a bucking horse. His plaid shirt appeared to be a comfortable match to his jeans.

Putting on a Stetson, he walked toward Ben and said, "I'll show you."

Outside, the man walked toward an old truck that had seen many prairie miles. "Get in," he said to Ben before the fellow took the driver's side. After Ben sat on the passenger's seat, a journey started.

"I know the Nelsons," said the man. "The older brother and sister arrived from the south. The sister married first and started a family. Later the brother also established a family. Although gradually they moved east, the homestead was maintained as a place for visiting. Later it was abandoned. On the site of the original house, there is a new home. The barn and chicken coup are in the process of returning back to the land. The Nelsons also owned property outside o' town. They had a cabin there. I have an old cabin across the road. My land borders the Kananaskis. I have cattle."

"Strange how I would meet the right person at the right time," observed Ben.

"Things like that happen a lot," said the man. "I'm Clint Nelson, the last of the western Nelsons. The others have moved east."

"Very pleased to meet you," exclaimed Ben. "I'm Ben Sands. "Do you know Calley Nelson?"

"Where do you think she gets her information about our family?" he replied. "She's my niece. She has been out here although I haven't been east. We also have corresponded with letters and emails. You know Calley?"

"When I got lost in a swamp, I found a homestead. I mentioned this to Calley who is a reporter and she said I had found the main story she had come south to locate. When we went to the site, we found items proving the homestead belonged to Charles and Winnifred Nelson."

"Isn't all this amazing," stated Clint. "As the years pass, I get more amazed by life. If I had known earlier what I know now, I would have tried to enjoy life more and see it as an opportunity rather than an ordeal. Too often we just go from one task to another without stopping to consider a wider view, seeing life's purpose that provides greatness and joy even in trouble. I regret I missed so much. If I'd known these things sooner, I could've seen more joy and beauty. Don't let this happen to you."

"I did not see life until I got lost in the Florida wilderness," observed Ben. "There I became lost no longer. Now, like you, I can see the wider view and this perspective erases defeat from trouble."

"That's why we have met," exclaimed Clint. "I learned from wilderness over many years what you derived all at once in Florida. I prefer your approach because you saw life when you are young."

"We are all the same age really," reflected Ben, "because we come here likely many times to learn by experiencing trouble since it does not exist in the spirit world that people sometimes call heaven."

"No one can ever tell me," exclaimed Clint, "that life is a random experience other than in our choices. The established part has no coincidences."

"We almost don't have to see the old homestead," declared Ben. "I have a hunch our meeting is why we are here."

"On days like this," stated Clint, "I can see that, although I have made mistakes I regret, I have stayed on the right course or I would not be on track to meet the trail marker that is our ride in this truck. We are aware we are not lost now. Our choices have been to continue on the journey with the Creator."

Stopping the truck, Clint said, "We are at the original Nelson homestead. We'll have a look around."

Leaving the vehicle, they walked to a gate in a fence. "You'll notice," said Clint, "the old place is returning to the prairie. A new home has been built on the previous house site. The Hopkins family lives here now. I know them well. They don't seem to be here now because their truck isn't here. The original chicken coup is that clump of boards to the left and obviously ahead is the fallen barn."

Running around the barn site, two horses came to the gate where Clint greeted them. "I know the horses too," he said as he held out two apples he had carried from the truck. Giving the horses the treat, Clint said, "I always have something for them. The apples are organic. There's no spray on them."

"I don't know anything about horses," admitted Ben.

"They're generally as friendly as we are," Clint replied. "That's likely the way life works for all living things." Starting to walk back to the truck, he said, "There's more to show you of the original Nelson homestead."

After driving along a gravel road, he turned down a two-lane track and stopped at another gate. "I own land on the other side of the road where I have a cabin," he explained. "The original, Nelson land beyond this fence has been sold. There was a cabin over by those cottonwoods," he added pointing to a stand of eight trees. "Little has changed here since the time when all of this area belonged to the Blackfoot who continue to have much surrounding land."

Both men observed the prairie where the almost constant companion of a breeze rustled across grass-covered hills. A coyote watched from a distant knoll. There was an eagle's nest in the cottonwoods and a hawk in the sky.

"Past generations on this land have a lot to tell us today but not enough people are listening," warned Clint as he gazed out over the prairie, seeing what could have been compared to the way things are. "People of the Blackfoot Confederacy have been here for countless years. Circular rings of stones outline locations where tipis have been. There are also larger stone circles where the people spoke to the Creator.

The first European settlers, the Nelsons among them, like the Blackfoot people, left no harmful mark on the land, leaving it much as they had found it. People today are causing destruction to the land that might never be repaired. The tar sands work is tearing up the environment, poisoning land, water, and sky. Fracking is poisoning our underground water. People here today don't want to see what the rest of the world now knows that green energy, particularly solar, is the future and also creates more employment. Present tar sands and fracking workers, making a lot of money, don't want to see beyond it."

"Are your views popular around here today?" asked Ben.

"No," he answered. "I'm the past and the future—not the present."

"I came here with an interest in finding the Nelson homestead because it completes my discovery of the first home in Florida," explained Ben. "However I have found so much more than the past."

"How's Calley?" asked Clint.

"She's a reporter in Florida," replied Ben. "She went south looking for the Nelson homestead. She was very pleased when I found it."

"You are part of our story," observed Clint, before he turned and started walking back to his truck. "Amazing," he added, "how life is connected."

"That's what I've discovered," agreed Ben.

They drove back to the center where they left the truck. Standing in front of the building, Ben said, "We traveled a long way in a short time. Thank you for taking the time to talk to a person who arrived here as a stranger."

"I thought maybe you weren't a stranger," replied Clint, "and I was right."

"You're a friend and I hope we'll talk more often," said Ben before turning to walk toward his car.

"Come back soon," said Clint before he entered the building.

Ben started the journey eastward. Amazing, he thought, how meeting Clint was like talking to someone I'd known all my life—and maybe I have.

Traveling eastward, he noticed how the prevailing wind from the west gradually gathered moisture, bringing increasing rainfall. Trees responded to larger amounts of water and forests gradually returned. I know where I'm going and what I'd like to do, he affirmed. I'll return to the wilderness where I'm lost no longer and I'll build a lodge. I assisted with the operation of the *End of the Road Beach Resort*. Having this experience, I'll build log cabins where people can visit to enjoy the wilderness. My new resort I'll call *End of the Trail Cabins*.

After arriving in the region of northern Georgian Bay in Ontario, he started searching. I know what I'm looking for, he reflected while his car moved past a familiar landscape of forests, rivers, and lakes. I've talked to people and checked out the land they have recommended. When what I'm looking for meets what I see, I'll be home. I want to find a place in the wilderness bordering Georgian Bay that is accessible by road. People from cities have been building cottages although most of these visitors have not moved as far north as I intend to locate. In the past, the only people who lived in remote areas where those who knew and were part of the wild. Recent years have seen wealthy, city people moving into wild places, not in a search for something but as an escape from hectic city life. Too often these visitors bring with them comforts and ideas of the city and push away the wild that is not understood and often feared.

I'm going to provide tourists an opportunity to not fear the wilderness but see it for its beauty beyond anything previously experienced because the natural environment was removed and paved over in the city. These people will have a vacation that even if for a short time will open them to greatness touching the sacred. Such a place will resonate with the life of each individual. They can then take this gift back with them so they will demand at home a green, healthy, living environment. City people will then stop destroying the wilderness, no longer seeing it as being in the way of progress, and will start bringing life of the wilderness and the beauty of the Creator's garden back to the city. That's my plan—my dream.

Occupied by his thoughts, Ben came to a road that was more of a lane. With heightened interest, he slowly, cautiously kept driving and declared to himself, maybe the *End of the Trail Cabins* will be at the end of this trail.

The car bumped across a vast swampy area leading to an elevated region that could almost be considered an island. Driving again on firm land, he came to an inlet of Georgian Bay. At the water's edge, there was a border of sand, backed by a grassy ridge next to the forest.

This is it, he exclaimed to himself as he looked around at an area that could not have been more perfect if his plans had been made with advance knowledge of this setting. I wonder, he mused, does this location match my dreams or did this spot form them. Either way, I'm home. I'll build cabins on the grassy border between beach and forest.

After purchasing the land, he bought two tents. Each one was large and heated by a wood stove. One would provide a storage area for tools including all necessary items such as saws, ropes, pulleys, and axes.

When the tents were established, he looked over his camp and decided, I'll build the log cabins myself then hire crews to do specialized tasks such as plumbing, electricity, propane fireplaces, windows, doors, and roofing along with well drilling. I'll also buy the logs.

My camp has been prepared, he noted as he checked the completed log outhouse at the back of two tents, one for tools and the other for living quarters. Looking inside his main shelter, he appreciated the comfort it provided for the approaching winter. Fir and hemlock boughs covered the floor while adding a fresh fragrance. Boughs were also used to form a mattress under the sleeping bag. Tables and chairs were located between a wood-burning stove at one end and a cooking area at the other. A propane-fueled stove supplied heat along with hot meals and drinks.

This tent is one part of my new home, he noted while enjoying a feeling of accomplishment. The tent containing tools is supplied with everything needed for construction. The logs have recently arrived.

Time has come, he concluded to look at the most important part of my home. In the wilderness, I am everywhere at home. When I was initially lost in the Florida wilderness, I struggled and fought back against the environment because it was an unknown stranger. Gradually I started to recognize the wilderness, not as an enemy but a spiritual world where there was harmony not found after people had either removed the wild entirely or just pulled out some threads such as apparently undesirable creatures or valued items including logs, gas, or oil. One strand's removal upsets the rest of the fabric and its original harmony. Various stages of chaos resulting from people's interference with nature are almost never seen as being caused by people. Blame is usually placed on the environment or some of its parts.

I will go for a walk, he concluded, to observe the rest of my home. At the water's edge, there is a small but natural sand beach. Back from it, on the grassy border in front of the forest, I'll build visitor's cabins along with one I'll use to replace the tents. My land is on an inlet from

Georgian Bay. On the east side, the shoreline is rocky and backed by forest. This section should provide some good bass fishing. The western part of the inlet is reedy and possibly a natural habitat for bass along with perch and pike. A creek enters the inlet on the west side. I'll explore upstream to check the back or southern region of my recently purchased land.

Starting to walk into the woods, Ben thought, I did not realize when I went for a holiday in Florida I was actually coming here. After getting robbed by two men who had been driving an old truck, I escaped from their bullets by running into the swamp. The part of my life they actually hit was my past life. I found my new life in the swamp. Previously it had been to me an unknown realm to be feared. Over time I became aware I was actually in the Creator's garden, having a spiritual connection in each part of the wild along with myself and other people who choose this path in life. Where once I saw an unknown terrain, I now see home where everything works in harmony and the most important connection—and value—is spiritual.

Continuing to walk southward, Ben said to himself, there is nothing more beautiful than undisturbed wilderness. Water in the creek is very cold. Likely there are trout here.

He followed the creek upstream to a small lake where with some fishing, he caught speckled trout. He roasted this food on a spit over a fire then dined well on trout accompanied by tea.

After enjoying a fine meal, he walked back to his tent. With night approaching, he settled into the sleeping bag. He was just about asleep when a whippoorwill called, sending clear, resonant sounds of wilderness ringing through the forest. After wolves howled, Ben slept soundly.

The next morning was greeted with a breakfast of pancakes and coffee before construction started. Dreams had become plans that brought supplies. Everything was ready for the hauling of logs along with cutting, chopping, and hammering. Cabins were started and floors finished. From these bases walls grew, leaving spaces for doors and windows. All cabins were completed together, each following the same process.

When the time came to finish the roofs much had changed. Another winter fully gripped the area. Birds and animals of the forest had time to learn that the person now living with them was not against them. Foxes had raised families from a den in a southerly facing sandbank. Always there was a pair of foxes in the area. They arrived to receive food set out for them. Ravens were also regular visitors who got food from a feeder. Only when nights were somewhat warmer, the raccoons appeared. Other regular occupants of the forest included beaver, deer, moose, mink, weasels, coyotes, wolves, and bears.

Snowshoe rabbits, like some of the other residents, acted like they hadn't seen people previously and did not know human hunters were the most dangerous strangers in the woods. Curiosity resulted and brought to the cabin sites visitors especially rabbits, deer, and moose. The area was generally moose country and there were less deer. Similarly, there were mainly gray, or timber, wolves, and a few coyotes. Foxes were not numerous. The construction work just happened to be taking place near a favorite den area and foxes started to be Ben's companions. He provided food to give them security. In return, they supplied company.

When Ben walked in the woods, one fox in particular, traveled with him. Actually, they were a pair but Ben called them both Red.

Sitting in his tent one morning, as he always did after breakfast and before going to work, he sipped coffee and observed life. I have been working almost four years now, he reflected. I have roughly completed eleven cabins. Ten are for tourists and the eleventh, at the eastern end, will be where I'll live. I enjoy working with wood. Logs, however, should not be cut from the wilderness. The least valuable part of a tree is a log. A wilderness tree has a larger life than wood. Such a tree is part of the Creator's garden and belongs with the wilderness that should not be reduced further or it will become endangered just like so many parts of its life.

The time has come, continued Ben, while enjoying another cup of coffee, to use wood only from trees that people have grown to be used for wood. In the same way, to get food and furs, wildlife should no longer be shot or trapped. Food, furs, and hunted animals now have to be produced on farms. There was a time when a small number of hunters could gather from the wilderness without wrecking it. Currently, the wilderness is the part that is small while hunters have become numerous. They have to be stopped from destroying what remains of the wild.

I have enjoyed constructing this lodge, mused Ben. I also savor this time of rest before starting the day's activities. I have worked for almost four years. I live with this forest. It is my home, making my residence so much larger than a tent or cabin. I just take trips to town to get supplies. The only food I get here is fish—trout or bass.

Maybe today, he concluded, I won't continue my usual routine. I have established the basic structures. The time has arrived to hire a crew to finish the resort.

He walked to the narrow strip of beach. First, he looked back at the tent that had sheltered him through the seasons while he built cabins for tourists along with one for himself at the east end to use as a home in addition to an office. My home is greater than a tent or cabin, he reflected again while looking at the surrounding forest bordering the inlet where sunlight danced on pure water. It was transparent at close range while gathering first some golden color from sunlight then adding shades of blue ranging from sky colors to darker hues at greater depths. He waded out then plunged into this cool, clear greenish-blue realm. The swim was refreshing, helping to clear away fatigue and soothe sore muscles.

Leaving the water, he sat down on a towel covering the sand while the morning sun brought warmth. After resting, he netted minnows, placed them in a bucket then packed them along with other equipment in his boat. He rowed to a reef at the entrance of the inlet.

With his baited line set near rocks below, he enjoyed the inlet's beauty with the reedy area to the west, rocky shore eastward, and a resort in the center next to the beach. The first strike on the bait sent a bass shooting out of the water amid a crest of spray.

After this first fighter and another were added to a stringer, Ben rowed back to his tent camp. In a short time, a special fragrance of frying bass fillets mixed with a constant scent of pine.

A meal was enjoyed consisting of bass fillets and fried potatoes followed by tea. While sitting in a chair next to coals of the outdoor fire, he watched the inlet that had drawn him to itself and revealed life of intricate workings where each segment fit in balance with others, establishing a song that when heard brought peace of such depth it could be recalled at any time for calm in adversity.

Feeling the calm, he recalled, in Florida I was at first lost and fought the menacing wilderness. Gradually, however, I let it in to change my life. With this awareness, I enjoyed the south while acquiring experience I've put to work here where I've let the northern wilds bring me in to enjoy and celebrate life. The new resort will be to provide other people with an opportunity to find what I've discovered. I will not rent cabins to hunters, trappers, loggers or other destroyers of the environment. The remaining wilderness is not for death but life. Tourists can come here to find it.

After opening a can of beer, he sipped it just as he saw the fox walk to a rock where food had been placed. Foxes have become my main companions along with ravens, raccoons, and chipmunks, he noted while enjoying the breeze drifting landward from Georgian Bay. The light wind was refreshing, warm and also carried with it a trace of scents from vistas of water and land. The main fragrance was of pine laced occasionally by a scent of fish.

Now that the wilderness has welcomed me to itself, my purpose is to build this lodge and have people come here to have an opportunity of finding rest so they can see more clearly what can be in their lives, reflected Ben. I have rested today and listened to forest silence. I now see I should go again to Florida and see what has happened to the *End of the Road Beach Resort*.

CHAPTER THREE

THE RETURN

After hiring a crew to finish the resort, Ben started a journey to the south. The drive gradually left the wilderness behind. Farms with their fields started to appear along with more roads, buildings, cities, and then an airport. The usual mixture of hurrying and waiting led to the plane. It seemed to remain motionless while only time passed until a gradual descent brought land into view along with a glimmer of sunlight brightening the Gulf of Mexico.

In a rental car, Ben welcomed the familiar landmarks of bridges and cities. At the location, where he had been robbed, he stopped on the side of the road. He got out of the vehicle and was greeted by warm humid night air. I came here for a holiday, years ago, he recalled while looking at the wilderness he had entered. I got a different holiday than what I expected. I entered the wild. More importantly, it entered me and that has made all the difference.

Driving again, he eventually welcomed a familiar landmark of the bridge over the Gulf Intracoastal Waterway. With growing excitement, he drove toward the resort that had become so much a part of his life. High expectations only led to disappointment.

The resort I came to visit has vanished, he told himself. In its place, there is a new establishment offering all conveniences and resembling all other places. There are more buildings—all larger—together with docks and boats. The past has gone—only to live now in memory of those with whom I shared this life. Hopefully, the wonderful reports written by Calley Nelson will hold indelibly the stories and prevent the footprints of our journey from being completely washed away, leaving behind only clear sand without the richness of our message.

Ben rented a room from a lady who talked without really seeing him. Yet she was efficient just like the room he entered. It has all the comforts for enjoying indoor life, he noted. Everything is supplied, like a machine dispensing supplies in return for cash.

He drove to the restaurant he had previously enjoyed visiting with Calley. It continued to be just as it had been, making the absence of Calley's company sharper.

Inside, after he sat beside a table, he welcomed the breeze entering through open windows facing the Intracoastal Waterway. A woman approached. She had black, medium length, graying hair. Her dark eyes and lined face indicated memories that would extend beyond Ben's recollection of the region.

"What would you like as a starter?" she asked.

"Draft please," he answered.

"Need a menu?" she asked.

"No," he replied.

"Didn't think so," she declared, seeming to have noticed he was not a stranger to the area.

"Grouper sandwich please—with cheese," he said.

"Always a good choice," she noted. "So's the cheese."

She walked away but returned quickly with the draft.

"Thank you," he said. "Pleased to see that this restaurant has not changed."

"We all are," she agreed. "There have been offers to make it newer and bigger yet that doesn't always mean better. We like the way it is and our customers seem to agree."

"This restaurant represents the coast of Florida and that's why everyone comes here," he observed.

"And I never tire of that," she confirmed. "The coast is always refreshing with a vibrancy brought from the wilderness of the sea. It can't be tamed—like parts of the shoreline."

"You should write a memoir," offered Ben.

"I am," she stated with eyes flashing. "I have a story to tell—not just about myself but of this land."

After she left, Ben sipped beer, letting it bring restfulness. The sandwich arrived.

Having enjoyed the meal, he paid his bill, added a good tip, and walked to the car.

Back at the resort, he went for a long walk on the beach. The Gulf has not changed, he observed. Maybe water quality and numbers of fish are different, yet the sea and part of the land continue to be a wilderness.

During the journey, he not only walked along the sand but in his memories he also returned to enjoy what he had found here during his previous visit. He could see again the old resort where he talked to Chuck Canby. Mainly there was Calley and the stories she had written.

Returning from a glimpse into the past, he entered the restaurant. Along one wall behind glass, there were copies of all Cal's stories along with pictures. They included accounts of the Nelson homestead in addition to artifacts found at the site. There was also the guy with the spear.

Ben ordered draft beer, sipped it slowly then returned to his room. He let sleep bring him to the dawn of the next day.

After breakfast, he savored coffee while sitting in a chair offering a view through windows to palms and the beach. Before I leave to go back to my new lodge, I have another memory to visit, he concluded. I'll rent a boat to see the other place where I lived. I'll go back to my shelter in front of the old Nelson homestead.

I hope I can find the site, he thought while slanting the rented boat's bow into small waves stirred by a warm, yet refreshing, breeze blowing in from the Gulf. Water occasionally splashed into the boat when a wave was hit at the wrong angle. The sky was cloud-strewn with no sign of a storm. A few pelicans flew overhead, constantly patrolling the water, looking for fish.

The journey continued until the resort had long ago been left behind. A small inlet appeared and Ben turned the craft toward it. I hope I get lucky, he thought before reducing the motor's speed. Maybe, just maybe, this is it, he exclaimed to himself as a patch of sand appeared. He steered for it then turned off the motor, allowing the momentum of the boat to carry it forward to the shore.

Moving to the bow, he stepped out onto firm sand. After tying the boat to a mangrove branch, he stood and looked closely at the area. I think I'm in the right place, he confirmed before following what appeared to be a path.

All my memories are more than dreams, he exclaimed to himself when he saw the shelter he had built years ago. He rushed forward, climbed the ladder, and sat on one of the chairs, going back in time to the sunlight of his best memories when he walked with a spear.

I must never forget what I learned here, he told himself. I'm now in a wave of remembrance, knowing this was a pivotal time in my life. I was tested and could have failed so completely my bones would now be back in the swamp. I'd be just one more missing person, among so many—another mystery. Instead, the forest enabled me to see another way. What was old became new again. I was pushed into a unique situation that made me look at life from a new angle and I saw what previously I had missed. The possibility was always there to see but each person has to choose. There's always a choice—stay on course or turn off the trail. I chose life and the Creator is life. That's all the opportunity of a successful life comes down to and the process is just that simple. Yet sometimes the right way is the hardest. Maybe that's why many people stray off the trail.

This chair I'm sitting on in this shelter, reflected Ben, has stirred all these thoughts. I'm back in time to one of my best circumstances in life yet everything good started with a robbery. Did the two robbers actually help me? That of course can't be true. Actually, they forced me into a desperate situation and I made the right choices.

Alarm flashed through him when he heard sounds of a person—or creature—climbing up the ladder. Following some scuffling, the top of a person's head appeared then a face. Shock gripped Ben when the individual's features came fully into view.

She stopped and stared while Ben looked into her eyes. They were pale brown. Her hair was slightly darker. The face held beauty and she said, "It's you. Ben?"

"Calley?" he gasped. "You're here?"

"You're here?" she whispered. "Or am I back in time—dreaming?"

"Both, really," he countered, as reality started to clarify.

She stepped into the shelter and said, "I can't believe it's you. When I come home I always walk around to look at the place. I saw the boat yet no one seemed to be present so I looked in the cabin."

"How did you get here?" he asked.

"My car," she answered. "I had a driveway put in. I bought this land using the money I made writing stories about you. I have a cottage back behind the homestead site. I don't get many visitors. They come sometimes by boat or car. Occasionally people who read my stories want to see the shelter and the homestead. I don't know what to do first to celebrate."

"You're here," he countered, still not quite believing what was happening. "You can't do better than that."

"You're back," she stated. "You can't imagine what a shock your presence is. I come to this shelter maybe once a day. Previously you've always been present but only in my memory. In my recollections and dreams, there's no passage of time. So in one way to have you present now is not a surprise. You never have left."

"I thought you had left," noted Ben. "I could not really relive my past here without you in it but I tried because you left to marry Carey Stiller."

"I didn't get married," she said after sitting down on one of the other chairs. "I came close. Always, though, there was a certainty that I would not go through with the plans."

"What happened?" he asked.

"Another guy," she said.

"That's not unusual," he added.

"The other guy was," she noted, smiling for the first time.

"You and Chuck Canby?" he asked, smiling.

"No," she replied, looking out the window that faced the Gulf. "He was the guy with the spear."

"Oh, that guy," confirmed Ben, almost whispering. "He changed my life too. I've never been able to forget him. He has stayed. I'm him now."

"That news is as good as seeing you again after these years," she exclaimed. "I have to—we have to—do something to celebrate. I'm going to the house and get beer for you and Margarita for me."

"Can I help?" he asked.

"Yes," she answered. "If I leave you, you might disappear again."

"That's why I want to help," he explained. "When you left the last time, you didn't come back."

"We'll both be keeping each other in sight for a while—until there's certainty the other won't leave," she stated.

"You're the reason I returned for another holiday although I tried to not keep thinking about you," he revealed.

"You're the reason I'm here—without Carey Stiller," she added. "He got married. Has a daughter."

After stepping down the ladder, they started walking back toward the homestead site when Ben said, "I got involved in a different way. I've been building a resort. It'll be finished by the time I get back. I'm calling it the *End of the Trail Cabins*."

"That's wonderful news," she exclaimed. "You're continuing your life at the *End of the Road Beach Resort*. I've kept my time with you too. I'm writing stories and novels."

"That's great news," he added.

"Here's the site you found," she said as they came to the homestead area. "Nothing's changed."

"Except your driveway and cottage," he observed.

"Yes," she agreed. "Maybe they aren't really changes so much as they are luxuries. More reliable to be able to drive here rather than come by boat. And a cottage helps get through the weather."

"Luxuries are hard to resist," he agreed. "You added a driveway and a cottage. A long time ago I left my new home in the swamp and walked to the *End of the Road Beach Resort*. I've built another resort."

"Maybe I could see that someday," she noted.

"I could be so lucky," he whispered.

"I'll show you what I've built," she noted, walking past the homestead site.

Opening the door of her cottage, she said, "The tour begins."

Inside, he exclaimed, "Your cottage is welcoming like a home should be—and yours would be. We are obviously in the living room with windows providing a view toward the Gulf. Lots of chairs, sofas, and a propane fueled fireplace."

"Sometimes a fireplace helps for warmth or burning off humidity," she explained. "There's also an air conditioner. The other rooms are of course a kitchen, washroom, two bedrooms and a computer room. The whole place is really an office. You notice the television too. I like watching news, weather, and movies."

"Good choices," he agreed. "A very welcoming and comfortable home."

"I'm too excited to cook," she observed. "Could I take you to the restaurant at the new *End of the Road Beach Resort*?"

"If that's your choice," he replied.

"It's a tough call between there or the other restaurant we liked," she considered.

"Your call," he repeated. "Both places are wonderful memories."

"Maybe the other restaurant we liked would be better because it hasn't changed," she suggested.

"Okay," he agreed. "Maybe I should get started with the boat and meet you there?"

"As long as you don't disappear again," she replied.

"And as long as you meet me at the resort," he added.

"Okay," she confirmed. "Maybe you should begin. Doesn't take long to get there by car."

"Good idea," he noted before leaving and quickly returning to the water. He rushed the trip to the dock where he returned the boat. Calley met him at the dock and they walked to her car.

"Maybe we should've celebrated in your shelter but that can come later," she suggested before they got into her car.

While driving, she observed, "I still can't believe you've come back. We maybe should've stayed at your shelter but I've too much energy to remain in one place."

"Restaurant's a good idea," he confirmed.

She parked her car on the lot facing the Gulf Intracoastal Waterway. A warm breeze was rippling the water as charter fishing boats along with a touring craft were returning to docks, marking the end of the day. Inside the restaurant, Calley selected the table where they had been previously.

The woman whom Ben had already met approached and said, "The fishing boats are coming in." To Ben, she added, "Your catch of the day looks like the best of them all."

"You're as smart as I thought you were the other time I was here," countered Ben, smiling.

To the woman, Calley said, "You could've said the same thing to me. Not really clear here who caught whom."

"Hopefully we're both sporting a hook," observed Ben, getting the women laughing.

"You're Margarita?" the woman asked Calley.

"Yes," she answered. "And Ben, you've met Rita?"

"Yes," he replied.

"Margarita and beer?" asked Rita.

"Maybe I'll celebrate today—and we could make that two Margaritas," noted Ben.

"Grouper sandwich with cheese and portobello?" asked Rita.

"Yes," answered Calley. "Smart people are a pleasure."

"You must have me confused with someone else," replied Rita with her face brightening.

"There's no confusion," countered Ben.

"Thanks," she said before walking away. She returned quickly with the drinks then left to greet other customers who had just arrived.

After sipping her Margarita, Calley asked Ben, "You had a Margarita before?"

"No," he replied. "But I hear it's made of tequila and I've had that in Mexico."

"I'd like to see Mexico someday," she said, ruefully.

"Okay," he answered and she smiled easily as her mood brimmed, joining Ben and all aspects of the moment in celebration.

"I have memories I visit when I dream," she said.

"I have too," he replied. "Speaking of memories, do you remember Clint Nelson?"

"Yes," she answered. "He is my uncle. I have visited him. Mainly we have corresponded. Most of our family history I have learned from him. Some day I would like to return and see him again along with the Nelson homestead in Claresholm, Alberta."

"I met him—and the homestead," he stated.

"You did?" she asked incredulously.

"Yes," he confirmed. "It was part of the story I wanted to see."

"I want to go back there for the same reason," she agreed. "That story is what set the hook for us—and the spear—the guy with the spear. That guy stopped me from getting married to Carey Stiller."

"Good," stated Ben. "That's the best thing the guy with the spear ever did."

"I agree," she exclaimed. "It would've been a mistake."

"I'm not good at saying this type of thing—actually makes me nervous—but do you think you could consider marrying the guy with the spear?"

"About time you asked," she replied. Raising her glass, as Ben did, she exclaimed, "To the future."

After finishing their drinks, Rita brought others and Calley said, "When I agreed to marry Carey, I was always worried. This time I was only worried that you had gone and were only a memory. I'll never forget the sight of you sitting in your shelter. Sometimes shining through the almost constant trouble, there are these glimpses that everything is right with the world—and our lives."

"Of all the things I've heard said," whispered Ben, "I've never agreed with anything more—and I see life the same way. At such times we see that we are lost no longer."

ABOUT THE AUTHOR

*D*aniel Hance Page is a freelance writer with twenty-six books published and others being written. His books are authentic stories filled with action, adventure, history, and travel including Native American traditions and spiritual insights to protect our environment in the smallest park or widest wilderness.

Made in the USA
Columbia, SC
07 May 2021